Praise for the Missing Pieces

"The Lavene duet can always be counted on for an enjoyable whodunit." — *Midwest Book Review*

"[A] terrific mystery series." — MyShelf.com

DAE'S CHRISTMAS PAST

"Paranormal amateur sleuth fans will enjoy observing Dae use cognitive and ESP mental processes to uncover a murderer...Readers will enjoy." ~ Midwest Book Review

A FINDER'S FEE

"The Lavenes once again take readers into a setting with a remarkable past, filled with legends and history...The characters are vivid and fascinating." ~ Lesa's Book Critiques

A HAUNTING DREAM

"I felt like I couldn't read fast enough on this one... but then I love all their missing pieces mysteries - can't wait till the next one. ~ Bookaholic

continued .

A SPIRITED GIFT

"This is the third book in the A Missing Pieces series. It's always enjoyable to visit Duck, NC and Mayor Dae and the interesting residents and this was no exception." ~ Fred Yoder

A TOUCH OF GOLD

"With a quaint coastal setting, a great cast and refreshing dialogue, this was an enjoyable and pleasant read and I look forward to reading the next book in this delightfully charming series." ~ Dru Ann Love

A TIMELY VISION

"Filled with likable (if eccentric) characters and boasts a vividly realized small-town setting. The combination of small-town ambience, a psychic main character, and plenty of antiques should give the authors plenty to work with in subsequent adventures." ~ Judy Coon for Booklist

. .

A Watery Death

By

Joyce and Jim Lavene

Book coach and editor—Jeni Chappelle

www.jenichappelle.com

Acknowledgement

With thanks to our granddaughter, Gabrielle Andreis,
for her rendering of Lilly the mermaid who brought
about this whole story! Love you!

Chapter One

Captain Bill Lucky swaggered down the Duck Shoppes boardwalk with his roving eye cast on every woman. They swooned at the sight of him.

He was an enviable man with his thick, slightly unruly black hair, and tall, commanding figure. Despite the heat of July in Duck, North Carolina, he wore tight black leather pants and a black leather vest over his blousy white shirt with hand-sewn French lace cuffs.

His leather pants ended in thigh-high black boots with gold chains on them. A filigree dagger of uncertain origin was tucked in the side of his right boot. Matching gold chains laced his vest.

"Ladies." He bowed gracefully as he entered the Missing Pieces Thrift Shop.

My friends, Trudy Devereaux and Reverend Lisa Wilcox, giggled when they heard his pleasant, sexy British accent. We'd been watching him as he approached.

Captain Bill Lucky was the entire romantic, masculine package. He was also Captain of the new gambling ship, Andalusia II, which sailed through the Graveyard of the Atlantic from Duck each night.

The ship was named for our local ghost ship that could be seen floating across the sea on moonlit nights. Its design had been taken from that famous lost galleon. The Andalusia was said to be the ghost of a wealthy Spanish treasure ship that foundered on the outer shoals like hundreds of others off the coast of Duck.

"Good morning," I greeted him, almost feeling the need to curtsy. "We were just having tea. Would you like to join us?"

"Indeed I would, dear lady." Captain Lucky kissed my hand and then set a red velvet bag on the floor near my burgundy brocade sofa, positioning himself carefully between Trudy and Lisa.

"I have Earl Grey, chamomile, and orange spice," I offered.

"Earl Grey sounds enchanting, Mayor O'Donnell. Thank you for offering."

He smiled at all of us, using his bright blue eyes to their best advantage. They had been likened to sunlit sapphires by the local gossips.

There was no doubt that the company that had built the gambling ship had made a wonderful choice to house this man in the captain's stateroom. He was attractive, personable, and a walking billboard for a romantic short cruise on the ocean. I wasn't sure if the ship even needed the hundreds of advertisements I'd seen in magazines. All they had to do was have him smile and invite people onboard.

I wondered what my ancestor, Rafe Masterson, would have made of Captain Lucky. Rafe was the scourge of Duck in his time, four hundred years ago. I decided that Rafe would've been happy with a gambling ship plying these waters. It would have sparked his interest.

"Thank you, dear lady." Captain Lucky gave me his most ravishing smile as I handed him his cup.

The four of us drank our tea. The shop was quiet the day before the big parade and festivities that came with the Fourth of July celebration in Duck. It was after that holiday that life got crazy for us.

During the off-season between November and June, there were barely six hundred full-time residents. The town set between the Atlantic and the Currituck Sound was pretty and quiet.

After June, we normally had an influx of twenty-five to thirty thousand visitors. The two lanes of Highway 12 that ran through the Outer Banks became clogged with traffic. Hotels and restaurants were full — that was a plus. Petty crime went up too, and that was a challenge for our tiny police department.

Since February when the gambling ship had launched, things had been different. There had been more people before the season, besides the hundred-and-twenty crew members who were there to service the vessel. The hotels had moderate gains, and most of the restaurants had stayed open. There weren't as many complaints from local people as when we had a full house in July, and the town was a lot livelier.

I wasn't looking forward to the crowds brought by the hot summer months.

Trudy was talking about her upcoming wedding. Her parents had purchased her custom-made gown from our local dress shop. It emphasized her slight figure and flawless, tanned skin. She was still unsure how to wear her platinum blond hair that day. Flowers were also in question.

Reverend Lisa would officiate at Trudy's wedding to my friend, Tim Mabry. She'd been a big help pulling the whole wedding together and working with my friends on their vows. It seemed as though the September date was coming up very quickly.

"If I may?" Captain Lucky entered the conversation with his usual suave style. "I believe every man wants to see his new bride with her hair flowing free. No clips or other unnecessary things. Just a wealth of silky mane, waiting for him to run his fingers through it."

He was as good as his word, running his long fingers through Trudy's shoulder-length hair.

She shivered, closed her eyes, and smiled. "Y-you really think so?"

"Very much so, lovely lady. I'm certain if you asked your betrothed he'd say the same."

Reverend Lisa smiled and ran her fingers through her own long, black hair. "I think Captain Lucky has a point, Trudy. And if any man knows about women, it's him."

I smiled and sipped my tea. Watching Captain Lucky's response was like watching the tide swell. He was a beautiful man, and he was well aware of it. But the times I'd spoken with him, he was also polite and seemed to be a genuinely nice person. I was never sure if that was part of the act or if it was really him.

"I have to go." Reverend Lisa got to her feet. "There's choir practice today and we have to be ready for the parade tomorrow."

"How is the float coming along?" I asked. The mostly tissue-paper-flower-covered truck bed had been accidentally left out and destroyed by rain two weeks before.

"It's much better." Lisa smiled. "We have some hardworking, talented people at our church. I've never seen tissue paper flowers fly out of scissors so fast. I'll talk to you later, Trudy. Have a good day, Captain Lucky. You too, Dae."

Trudy left too. She had to get back to her shop, Curls and Curves Beauty Spa, next door. She winked and pursed her lips at leaving me alone with Captain Lucky. She didn't have to worry about anything going on between us. I would never be Captain Lucky's type.

I put her flowered cup and saucer back on the small sideboard that I used for making tea at the shop. Friends tended to drop by, and I always wanted to be ready for a nice chat. That was part of why Missing Pieces was so important to me.

For my grandfather who shared a house with me, Missing Pieces was a place that I could put all the things that came to me. I had a gift for finding things — never useless things but sometimes things that had to be kept for a while to understand their value. It took some people time to realize what they'd lost, and why it was important.

Of course some of what I kept and sold in my little shop belonged to no one. Or I'd come across it when people had needed or wanted to sell something. Even those things required someplace to be until they'd found a new home.

As I was rinsing the cups and saucers, I realized that Captain Lucky hadn't left. He'd bowed to Lisa and Trudy as they'd walked out the door, but he'd stayed behind, perusing everything I had for sale.

I dried my hands on a towel and smiled at him. "Are you looking for something in particular?"

"No. Not exactly." He smiled back at me and adjusted the chains on his vest.

Of course. The red velvet bag.

"You have something to sell?"

His face turned a little pink, but even embarrassment looked good on him.

"Yes. I'm a little short of cash, and I thought you might be interested in an item. It's one of a kind. Very unique."

I walked to the front, glass counter where I kept small, very valuable items under lock and key. "I'll be glad to take a look. No promises."

"No. I certainly didn't expect any." He retrieved the red velvet bag and joined me at the counter. "I believe you'll be interested in this item. Believe me — I would never part with it if it weren't necessary."

He opened the velvet bag with a flourish, like a stage magician about to unveil something that would surprise and amaze me. Inside was a single piece of white coral that had been carved into the shape of a small cornucopia.

Captain Lucky held it out to me. "My ancestor sailed with Christopher Columbus when he found the New World. My great-grandmother was from Genoa.

She claimed that he was related to us. That's how the horn came to be in her hands. She gave it to me on her deathbed as her only heir."

I was reluctant to take the piece in my hands without wearing protective gloves. Part of the way I was able to find missing or lost items was to hold hands with their owners. I could also touch something and see its history — where it had been and sometimes where it was going. I could tell many fascinating secrets about people and their belongings.

Sometimes those secrets were terrible, painful memories that were trapped in the item. That had happened to me too many times not to be prepared for the worst.

"Is something amiss?" he asked as he watched me put on my gloves. "I assure you that the horn doesn't hold germs or diseases, if that worries you."

Captain Lucky was new to Duck. Local residents knew about my gift for finding lost things and people. They'd grown accustomed to the times when I felt the need to protect myself.

"I'm not worried about germs," I assured him. "But sometimes my gift can be painful. Bad memories can be left behind in things that come to me. They cause harsh disturbances."

He looked surprised at that, his blue eyes between thick black lashes widening for a moment. "I had no idea. I've heard the tales about you, of course. You've found people who were kidnapped and missing objects that might never have been located. I didn't know those things made an impact on your life in that way."

"I just need a little protection sometimes." I felt silly hearing him say the words back to me. "Better safe than sorry, my grandfather always says."

"And a good axiom it is too." He put his hand on mine. "I'm sorry. I didn't mean to embarrass you. If you feel you need protection to examine this for me, I understand."

Sometimes I got immediate impressions from people when they touched me. Captain Lucky was one of those people. I could see what he'd had for dinner yesterday—shrimp—and knew he'd been kissing someone right before he came here today. I couldn't see the lady's face, but it didn't surprise me, and I tried not to judge.

He seemed more nervous to me than shrimp or a kiss would make him. I wondered if it was because of the item he wanted to sell or the reason he felt it was necessary to sell it.

"That's all right. It's no bother. And what an interesting piece this is, even without your family's story that goes with it. You called it a horn. What does it do?"

He chuckled. "I can't speak to it myself since I've never witnessed it, but my great- grandmother swore that a mermaid gave it to my ancestor on his voyage. It seemed she had fallen in love with him and wanted to have a way to contact him. No cell phones at that time."

As he spoke, I examined the coral horn. It was amazingly light, and so carefully hewn that all the edges were round and perfectly smooth. It twisted upon itself like a conch shell with several layers leading to the center of it. Inside, the white coral had a pink tone that reached to a deeper purple at its heart.

"What happened to your ancestor?"

"Alas, I have no idea. I assumed he made it home

on his last voyage since we have this fine work of art. I'm not even sure what his name was, as my great-grandmother had forgotten."

"And what was he supposed to do with it?"

Captain Lucky lazily grinned, showing perfect white teeth. "Why blow it, of course. The horn is supposed to summon the seafolk, one mermaid in particular. My great-grandmother warned me never to blow into it. She said people had told her the result of calling the seafolk could be cataclysmic. Thus, I have never tried it. The people in Genoa, who live and die by the sea, know about these things."

Even through the gloves, I could feel an energy coming from the horn. It didn't feel dark or angry, but there was power there. It was probably best that Captain Lucky had never tried to use it.

I put the horn back in the velvet bag and took off my gloves. "I could never pay you what this is worth. I'm sure a collector would give you quite a bit for it with the provenance you have."

He put his hand on the bag. "How much could you give me for it now, Mayor?"

There was that edge again.

"I don't know. I could take a look at what I have. It's more likely that I'd have a better cash supply after the parade tomorrow when tourists hopefully swarm into my shop and buy everything." I smiled at him to keep it light, but his frown deepened.

"There is a certain problem that has arisen for me. I hesitate to burden you with it, but I find myself at loose ends and needing to get out of town for a few days."

In other words, he needed the cash now.

It wasn't the first time someone local had brought

me a valuable artifact that they wouldn't have parted with except in an extreme situation. I wasn't a pawn shop, but I'd held things for people before who'd come back for them with the money I'd paid them in hand.

I looked in the register. I'd had a sale that morning—a good one—and for once had more than a few dollars. My business wasn't big enough for me to keep a stash of money for these particular times. Some months, I was barely able to pay rent and utilities.

"There's five hundred dollars in here," I told him. "If that will help you—"

"Bless you, lady mayor." Captain Lucky seemed thrilled with that amount. "That should suffice my needs until my next payday. I shall have returned by then. I am very grateful to you."

"I won't sell it," I told him. "It will still be here when you come back."

Captain Lucky was near tears after my words. He lifted my hand in his and lingered over it, planting a soft but endearing kiss on it. "I am forever in your debt. If it were not for my knowledge of your fiancé being a potentially dangerous man, I should spirit you away from him!"

Between the kiss and his deep, soulful gaze on my face, it was no wonder that my fiancé, Kevin Brickman, had a curious expression on his face when he stopped by to pick me up for lunch.

"He's very grateful," I explained to Kevin.

"I can see that." His lips twisted in a wry smile. "Good to see you, Captain Lucky. If you're done with my girlfriend's hand, maybe you'd like to join us for lunch at Wild Stallions."

Captain Lucky released me and accepted the five

hundred dollars in cash that I gave him.

He quickly shook Kevin's hand. "It's very good to see you, innkeeper. Your lady has made my morning a celebration. You are indeed a fortunate man."

Captain Lucky nearly skipped out of the shop and down the boardwalk.

"What was that all about?" Kevin asked.

"He said he needs to get out of town for a few days. He was willing to give away a family heirloom for five hundred dollars." I carefully took out the horn, with gloved hands, and laid it on the velvet bag. "I'll give him his horn back after he gets paid. I'm not sure if I could sell it anyway. It has an interesting story that goes with it. If it's true, it could be worth thousands of dollars."

He lifted the coral horn and examined it. I told him about Captain Lucky's family ties to Christopher Columbus.

"You wore gloves when you looked at it, right?" He put it back on the bag.

"I wouldn't take a chance with it."

The door opened, and Mrs. McGee came in with a blast of warm wind from the Currituck Sound—not to mention her precocious grandson, Travis.

"She's only here for a package," I whispered to Kevin. "Just a minute and I'll close for lunch."

"No rush."

Mrs. McGee took her package and told me all about the special event her Girl Scout troop had planned for the next day. I didn't notice when Travis lifted the coral horn and fixed his lips to it as though he knew exactly what to do.

Before I could stop him, he blew into the coral. A

long, mournful sound came from it that echoed for several minutes. The hauntingly deep call took over every other sound. It was as though nothing else moved until it had faded away. Time stood still.

And then it was gone.

Mrs. McGee apologized and took the horn from Travis but not until a shiver of warning had rippled through me.

Chapter Two

"So you think he called the seafolk to shore?" Kevin chuckled after we'd ordered lunch at Wild Stallions. The restaurant was a short walk from Missing Pieces along the boardwalk past Duck General Store and Mrs. Roberts' Pet Emporium.

"I felt something when he blew it." I took a sip of water. "I hope it wasn't anything bad."

"I don't think there are any seafolk out there," Kevin said. "It's a good story, but no one has ever really seen a mermaid."

Kevin Brickman was a wonderful man who I loved deeply. He understood my gift, sometimes better than I did since he'd worked with psychics during his time with the FBI. He was open to almost anything that involved abilities the mind could produce—but he was a little light on folklore.

"We've had several sightings of seafolk in Duck history," I told him. "I think I remember even seeing a sketch of a mermaid at the historic museum."

I looked into his ocean-colored eyes, more gray than blue. His mouth still had the hard lines I'd first noticed about him. But time in Duck as the owner of the Blue Whale Inn had softened him. The trace of sadness that had haunted him, causing him to leave the FBI, was gone. It was replaced by a tan and strong smile lines. He was tall and fit from working on the maintenance of the old inn that had become very popular again since he'd reopened it.

"There are also drawings of sea serpents at the museum," he said with a smile. "I wouldn't put much stock in those renderings either."

"There is more in heaven and earth, Horatio," I quoted.

Our wine and glasses of ice water arrived, and the debate ended as Kevin changed the subject.

"Have you given any thought to our engagement party?" he asked. "I'm only asking because everyone keeps asking me."

"I've thought about it." I sipped my wine. "The problem is that Trudy and Tim are getting married in September. You know how everyone in Duck has thrown a party for them. I'm so busy trying to get everything set up for *her* wedding. I just don't want to step on her big moment."

He nodded. "That makes sense. I'll tell anyone who asks that we're being polite about our engagement so Trudy and Tim have a good wedding."

"Are you okay with that?" I touched his hand.

"I suppose I have to be, right?" He took my hand in his. "What do you pick up from me?"

I closed my eyes and aligned my thoughts with his. "I see that you have a big order of shrimp coming from Charleston today."

Kevin laughed. "Good to know you can't see *everything* about me."

I laughed too, as lunch arrived.

It was surprising how easy it had become to know what was going on with people around me, especially those I knew well. When I was a child, I had learned quickly that I could hold someone's hand to find missing items they were looking for. Gramps and my mother had encouraged me.

They knew all the good things my grandmother, Eleanore, had done with her gift. But she'd died before I was born — or at least that was what I'd been told.

The more I used my gift, the stronger it became. Now I could see other things about the people I chose to read. I could also pick up items and know everything about them.

Sometimes what I saw in people and their belongings wasn't pleasant. On the other hand, I had helped people. I still thought of my gift as the ability to find missing pieces — just like the shop. The hard part was finding the right place for each piece.

I'd seen something else when I held Kevin's hand.

He was upset about not being able to share our relationship with his family. He was thinking about his parents and brother who lived in Maryland. They hadn't come to visit him yet and seen the remarkable things he'd done with the old inn.

Kevin wanted them to meet me too. I knew he wasn't close to his family. He rarely spoke of them and hadn't seen them for years.

We didn't talk about that. I didn't want him to feel like he couldn't keep something from me. Instead, we talked about the parade the next day, and the renovation of my heavy, old-fashioned mayor's coat.

"I'm sure if Darcy has taken off about fifty pounds on that coat, it will fit you right," he said.

"It wasn't made for me. I'm sure Mad Dog had it made for him since he expected to be the first mayor of Duck after incorporation."

He touched a strand of my sun-bleached brown hair. It was always a bit windblown, no matter how hard I tried to keep it neat.

"Why wasn't Mad Dog the first mayor? I know the town appointed you. Why didn't they pick him?"

I shrugged. "Gramps was sheriff back then. He had a big reputation and had worked hard to bring about the town's incorporation to fight off the big hotel that had wanted to build on the Currituck Sound. He has at least as many friends as Mad Dog. Gramps wanted me to be the first mayor. I guess that's why they picked me."

Mad Dog was Randal 'Mad Dog' Wilson. He was from one of the founding families of Duck, just like my family, the O'Donnells.

He was a mountain of a man — tall and broad — who was used to getting his own way. He had once been a popular race car driver and had spent several years on the town council.

He'd run against me for the mayor's spot last year and lost. That meant he'd lost his seat on the council too and had subsided to simply being a problem about everything that went on in town.

"Well even if the mayor's coat seems too big for you, sweetheart, the job fits you well. I can't imagine a better official for this town." Kevin smiled and lightly kissed me.

"Thanks. You know I love my work, and getting that salary is nice too."

The town council had voted to give me a small salary now. It wasn't enough to live on, but it was enough to help me through the lean months over the winter when the shop didn't make much money.

"Of course it was decent of them to give themselves salaries too."

I didn't comment on that. The town had the money for it. The salaries weren't huge. I didn't feel bad about it, though it had been controversial.

Lunch was delicious, as always. Cody Baucum stopped by our table to ask how everything was. He and his brother, Reese, owned Wild Stallions. Reese and Cody were similar in appearance—medium height and build, sandy brown hair and brown eyes. Some people had a hard time telling them apart even though they weren't twins.

Cody had become a town council member during the last election. He'd had dozens of great ideas so far. I believed he'd be a huge asset to Duck as we continued to grow. It was good to have someone under fifty on the council besides me.

"I don't know about you, but I'm not looking forward to the council meeting tonight." Cody refilled our water glasses. "Mad Dog and a few other people are bringing a petition to close down the gambling ship."

"You're kidding. I thought we were over that and everyone loved having the extra money it brings in in."

He shrugged. "I'm sure merchants like it. I like it. How about you, Kevin?"

"What's not to like? The Blue Whale Inn is always full. That's good for me."

"It's the extra traffic on the roads," I explained. "Everyone has been at Missing Pieces complaining about it. There's also the problem with extra criminal activity, just like Sheriff Riley warned. Residents don't like it."

Cody agreed. "Chief Michaels said he arrested twenty shoplifters last month. That's a record for us, even over the summer. He and Sheriff Riley are behind Mad Dog on getting rid of the gambling ship."

"It should be an interesting conversation," Kevin said. "In my experience, it's not easy to get rid of something you've already allowed."

I knew Kevin was right. The nervous council members had discussed it. It might only be people who lived here full-time who didn't like the gambling ship, but they were the people who voted.

Cody said he'd see us later and headed toward the kitchen.

"So when is the next wedding party?" Kevin asked. "We're not hosting it at the Blue Whale."

"That's because it's at Trudy's grandmother's house in Kill Devil Hills. I think the one after that is at her aunt's house."

"And when is *our* first engagement party?"

"Right after Trudy leaves on her honeymoon." I smiled at him as I got my things together to leave. "Do you want to host it at the inn?"

Kevin got his credit card back from the cashier, and we left Wild Stallions.

"That's fine." He took me in his arms as we stepped out on the boardwalk. There was a small, secluded corner beside the restaurant locally known as Lover's Nook. "And when are you moving in with me?"

He kissed me, and I waved to several Duck residents who laughed at us hiding in Lover's Nook like a couple of teenagers.

"After the wedding?" I wasn't quite sure about that part.

I wanted to marry Kevin, but I felt bad leaving Gramps alone at the house. I knew he could take care of himself, but he'd never lived alone. He was born and raised there. My mother hadn't left home when she'd found out she was pregnant with me. Then my grandmother died, and my mom and I lived there with him. Now there was only him and me.

"I don't have to be gifted to know that you're not telling me everything," Kevin half joked. "What's wrong, Dae?"

"It's nothing," I told him with a big kiss. "I should get back to the shop. This is my biggest weekend, you know. I don't want to miss an important sale."

Kevin walked back to Missing Pieces with me but didn't bring up anything else about us getting married or moving in together. I was glad, since I had no ready answers to why I was troubled about leaving Gramps.

It was probably just pre-wedding jitters. Trudy had been worried about all kinds of crazy things while we'd been planning her wedding.

We parted with another kiss and a long hug at the open door, until a customer brushed by us and went into the shop.

"I'll see you later. I love you, Dae."

"I love you too, Kevin." I watched him walk down the boardwalk, troubled by our conversation and something more. I could feel a prickling of something about to happen between my shoulder blades.

It was hot, and the air-conditioning was on, but I wished I could leave the door open as I did spring, fall, and winter. The breezes from the sound were always pleasant, but the back of the shop got hot and humid if the door stayed open too long. Most customers didn't like lingering to look things over in that kind of environment.

A few customers came and went in quick succession. I was alone again and sorry that I'd sent Kevin away. Maybe we could've talked out the problem about the wedding. There might be an answer that I wasn't seeing about Gramps. But I knew Kevin was busy at the inn too. We'd talk later.

Since I wasn't busy, I lifted the coral horn that I'd stashed in the locked glass case until I could put it away. I didn't want any other children, or adults for that matter, blowing into it again.

I realized where that odd feeling had begun—the horn. I also hadn't put on my gloves to handle it. Big mistake as the memories and feelings trapped in it hit me like a tidal wave.

Deep in the deepest parts of the sea. Swimming through the cool water.

Her heart belonged only to one man. Where was he? Why didn't he call her?

She was so alone. There were many others of her kind, but her mind saw only him.

If she could find him again, she would never let him go.

"Excuse me, miss?" An older gentleman was staring at me. He held a pirate carving in his hand. "Are you all right? Could I get a price on this?"

I shook myself out of the place I had gone.

A mermaid's heart.

"I'm sorry." I staggered and slurred my words like a drunken woman. "Of course. That's a carving of our most famous pirate, Rafe Masterson, Scourge of Duck." I named a price.

The man in the green-checkered shorts whistled and hastily put the figure down. "Too high for me. Thanks."

Sinking down on the stool behind the cash register and case, I took a few deep breaths. I could feel every beat of the mermaid's heart. Her sorrow was terrible. I could see the water around her, the sunlit ocean with thousands of fish swimming through it.

I flexed my feet, still feeling her tail.

Quickly, I put on my gloves and got the velvet bag to put the horn away. It was real. There were seafolk, just as the legends had claimed.

While I was letting that sink in, something hit the floor—keys—a house key and a car key.

Captain Lucky's keys?

They had to be. I knew he lived on the ship. Maybe it was the key to his stateroom and his car.

Everyone in Duck had Captain Lucky's cell phone number. I looked up his cell number in my phone and gave him a call. No answer. The phone rang until it finally went to voicemail.

I tried texting him, but there was no response to that either. I looked at the time. He must not have noticed that he'd left his keys. He'd probably come here in the ship's golf cart or walked. That was how most people in Duck traveled.

He'd said he was leaving. I drummed my fingers on the glass cabinet. He'd probably need his keys. Whatever he was trying to get away from hadn't sounded like it could wait. I knew I'd have to take his keys to him.

Gramps arrived at just the right moment.

"Hi, honey. Just stopping to let you know I won't be home for supper. I've got a hot charter in thirty minutes. Should be good money to put into the fund for repairing the back porch."

My grandfather, Horace O'Donnell, owned a charter fishing boat. He took tourists out on expeditions in the sound almost every day, except Sunday. It was a far cry from his previous job as Dare County Sheriff, but I was glad he'd decided to retire. Being sheriff had taken its toll on him. I could see it in his faded blue eyes and thinning white hair.

Now instead of wearing his brown sheriff's hat, he wore a green fisherman's cap with hooks caught in it. He usually wore a red rag around his neck, brown shorts with dozens of pockets, and a brown T-shirt that advertised for his charter service.

"You're a life saver." I picked up Captain Lucky's keys as I put the horn away again. "I have to run these over to the Andalusia. Can you watch the shop for me? Is the golf cart in the parking lot?"

"Sure." He didn't sound sure. "I could just take them over there for you."

"You could," I agreed. "But I don't want Captain Lucky to think I told everyone about his keys and our business together. You know how it is."

Everyone who had ever lived in Duck knew that it was a hive of gossip. Sometimes it could be hurtful. Captain Lucky might be down on his luck. Everyone didn't need to know.

"Okay. You're right. But what do I say when people ask where you are?"

"Make something up," I told him.

"You know I'm the world's worst liar, Dae. Tell me what to say."

I thought a minute. "Tell them I had to go help Kevin with some shrimp. I'll be back before you know it."

Gramps scratched his head. "Just don't make me late for my charter."

Several customers streamed through the door. It was all I could do not to go back and take care of them. But Gramps knew what to do. He'd substituted for me plenty of times.

I left the boardwalk quickly, pleased to see plenty of cars parked in the lot behind the shops. There was a full crowd at the coffeehouse and bookstore in the parking lot too. It was great to have thousands of tourists show up for our Fourth of July celebration.

Gramps's golf cart was parked close to the stairs. There wasn't any designated parking for golf carts, even though there were probably more golf carts in Duck than cars. Dozens were jammed together in a knot that was going to make it difficult to get out for the two carts at the center of it.

Of course it was easy to find Gramps's cart because

it wasn't one of the plain, open ones. His had a roof on it and sides that could be closed in case of rain. It was also squarely parked in an open parking space—taking up one of the limited spaces for cars—no doubt an issue that would be brought before the town council at some point.

I got in and started it up. There were several unhappy frowns from car drivers who didn't like golf carts taking their spaces. I waved and pulled out quickly. Everyone had a right to a safe place to park as far as I was concerned.

Duck Road separated the Shoppes on the Boardwalk from the road that ran to the Atlantic Ocean on the other side of town. The road dead-ended at the Blue Whale Inn and the house that had been donated for the Duck Historical Society by Miss Elizabeth Simpson.

There were hundreds of people in bathing suits and shorts walking the main roads. Traffic was snarled as always on the barely two-lane streets that ran through town. I had to wait ten minutes to get across and then had to zigzag through the walkers and runners.

This was peak season for us—which meant very few vacancies in vacation home rentals. In the other three seasons, this road would be empty most of the time. Even the gambling ship hadn't come close to bringing in as many people as hot summer days and the promise of a golden beach.

Kevin waved as I passed the loading area behind the Blue Whale. I'd helped him paint the old inn when he'd first arrived. He'd done significant upgrades to the three-story building that had stood empty for a generation. Now it was popular with visitors and people in town again. Kevin had put in a gorgeous arbor by the sea where Trudy and Tim were going to be married.

I could see the tall masts of the Andalusia II long before I reached the impressive pier and waiting area a few blocks down from the Blue Whale. The company had gone to great expense to accommodate gamblers who came from all over the world.

The waiting spot was a quaint tavern that was designed to resemble something from the 1600s, only with air conditioning, heat, and Wi-Fi. There were snacks and drinks available with an entire wall of glass to get a good view of the ocean and the magnificent ship. The pier went out seven-hundred feet into the gray/blue water. The ship was berthed here between journeys out to the legal limit where guests could gamble.

But the whole enterprise was anchored by the impressive replica of the Spanish treasure ship that went down in a fierce storm in 1720 with all hands lost. The people of Duck—known as Bankers—had lived off its spoils for years. Not all the treasure had been retrieved, even though hundreds of people, through present day treasure hunters, had searched for it.

"Hi, Dae!" Barney Thompson's daughter, Celia, worked at the ticket office. "What brings you down here?"

"Is Captain Lucky on the ship? He left his car keys at my shop this morning." I knew how that was going to sound before I said it, but I had to explain why I wanted to see him.

Celia's deep brown eyes grew wide in her round

face. "You and Captain Lucky? What happened to Kevin Brickman?"

"Captain Lucky and I aren't dating," I explained. "It was just a fluke. He was at Missing Pieces and dropped his keys. I want to return them before he needs them."

"I can't believe you'd abandon Kevin. Weren't you guys going to get married?"

There was no pretty way out of this. "We *are* getting married, Celia. Right after Trudy and Tim. Captain Lucky was at the shop. That's all."

"Really?" She lowered her voice suggestively — as if I hadn't said anything. "So you're just fooling around with Captain Lucky, right? I never pictured him as the type to settle down. You're right to have him as your boy-toy. Kevin is handsome and stable, even if he is a little old."

Celia was eighteen, just out of high school. At that age, Kevin approaching forty looked ancient. Me too, probably.

"So is it all right if I take Captain Lucky's keys out to him?" I tried to get the conversation back to my original question.

"Oh, sure. There isn't another tour until four. You should be able to catch the courier going out there with supplies and hitch a ride. See you later, Dae. I hope you're inviting me to your wedding. And don't worry about Kevin. He won't hear anything about Captain Lucky from me."

"Thanks, Celia." But I didn't believe a word of it. At least everyone would only be talking about me and Kevin, not about Captain Lucky's need to get out of town for a few days.

She was right about the courier. He was on a golf cart and pulling a wagon with sides behind him. The cart was full of liquor boxes and the driver explained that their order at the local ABC liquor store had been shorted.

"I don't want to be at sea with a bunch of people losing money and no alcohol," he joked.

He said his name was Jet. He wasn't from Duck but was there for the summer to work. He was a handsome young man with bronze shoulders barely covered in a tight, white tank top.

"I like this area, even though it's small." He looked out at the horizon where the sky was clear. "I can't imagine living here. My friend who invited me down for the summer grew up in Duck. I don't know if he plans on staying now that he's out of school."

"I suppose if you like big towns, this would be disappointing," I agreed as we went quickly down the pier to approach the boarding ramp that led up to the ship. "Who's your friend who grew up here?"

"Dale Fargo. You know him?" Jet smiled at me, one hand on the wheel.

"Sure. His mother is the fire chief. I remember Dale."

He backed the cart up to the ramp, a plain word for an elaborate, wide, entry that went to the Andalusia II. It was decorated with pirate paraphernalia, which had seemed odd to me on the replica of a Spanish treasure ship. The Spanish hated the pirates as much as anyone else. But the pirate theme—including Captain Lucky's outfit—was prevalent onboard.

The gambling company that had built the ship probably found the pirate look more interesting and didn't care about the history.

I helped Jet with a few of the liquor boxes. He called for other crew members to help with the rest. The first mate, an interesting man wearing 17th century Spanish garb, greeted me as I went onboard.

"Mayor O'Donnell." The handsome first mate did a sweeping bow in front of me with his feathered hat in hand. He wasn't as charismatic as Captain Lucky, which was probably why he was first mate.

"Mr. Lynch." I shook his hand. Carl Lynch was a new member of our community. He'd moved to Duck expressly to be on the ship. "It's good to see you."

He kissed my hand, his dark head hovering over my arm for several minutes, making the other crew members walk around us as they moved boxes of liquor to the bar area.

"To what do we owe this pleasure? Will you be sailing with us, ma'am?"

"No. I came to see Captain Lucky. They told me he was here."

"Of course. Come right this way." He tucked my arm into his and smiled. "May I offer you refreshment?"

"I'm kind of in a hurry, thanks. The captain's quarters are this way, if I remember correctly. I can go by myself. I'm sure you have better things to do."

His very dark eyes were wide in his chocolate-colored face. "Better things to do than to escort my lady mayor to the captain? I think not. Allow me to show you there."

I didn't argue with him. It was interesting watching all the activity that went on before the ship was set to sail. Dozens of crew members were making sure all the brass-plated rails were shining. A pirate ship, or a Spanish galleon, never received this kind of attention in real life.

"We've ordered new slot machines, if you'd care to take a look below deck," he invited. "They have a pirate theme, and pay off in replicated gold doubloons."

"Thanks, no. Maybe some other time."

"You'll find our menu has improved as well. We're offering more than just seafood now for dinner, and we have a live band every night. We have Tom Mason and the Blue Buccaneers tonight. I'll bet you love them, right?"

"I do enjoy their music. I've never seen them in person."

He jumped on my revelation and gave me a free supper tour pass.

"I hope you'll take advantage of it."

"Thank you." I put the pass in my pocket. We were right in front of the captain's large quarters at the other end of the hundred-foot ship. "I'll knock, if that's okay."

"Oh, no. Allow me."

Mr. Lynch rapped smartly at the beautiful inlaid doors that opened into the cabin. There was no response at first. He knocked again, but still no answer.

One of the crew arrived with a case of brandy on his shoulder. "This is for the captain, Mr. Lynch, if you and the lady wouldn't mind moving out of the way."

The crew member rudely barged between us and pushed open the double doors. We prepared to follow him into the cabin, until we heard a stifled scream and the box of brandy fell to the heavily-carpeted floor.

"Madre de Dios!" Mr. Lynch turned to stare at the elegant cabin. "What happened here?"

Chapter Three

The captain's stateroom was large, occupying one full end of the ship. Captain Lucky was expected to entertain special guests lavishly in this space. It was meant to impress.

Heavy, wood-paneled walls were accented by brilliant tapestries and paintings. Brightly colored Tiffany lamps hung from the ceiling, also occupying a space on a wide oak desk and on an intimate dining table with four red velvet-covered chairs.

There was no other room onboard that was more opulent than this one. Everything here was handcrafted and richly appointed. It was meant for a man of power and influence.

In this case, it had been created for Captain Lucky,

the first skipper of the Andalusia II. And he was there, sprawled in his usual tight leather, a final look of pain and fear on his handsome face.

"What should we do?" The crew member picked up the box of brandy with trembling hands. "Shall I fetch the ship's surgeon?"

"I don't think the surgeon can help Captain Lucky now." Mr. Lynch moved quickly to the bed and touched a hand to the captain's throat. "As I thought— he's dead."

"We should call Chief Michaels," I advised. "They'll want to send someone out here."

"But what's all this stuff?" the crew member asked. "This wasn't here when I came in yesterday."

Mr. Lynch stroked a hand across what looked like seaweed, dragging some down. It hung from the lights and the tapestries, and was spread across every surface. "I don't know."

I was so stricken seeing Captain Lucky that I hadn't realized until that moment that the thick carpet underfoot was soaked with water. As my feet sank into it, it made a squishing sound. "The whole room is wet."

"This is crazy." The crew member backed toward the door. "How did it get this way? Is the ship sinking?"

"Don't be daft, man," Mr. Lynch practiced his brand of historical speech. "Of course the ship isn't sinking. Check the window. Maybe it's broken and water came in."

"I'm not checking anything, man." The terrified crew member sprinted out the door, shouting that Captain Lucky was dead.

"Get back here!" Mr. Lynch yelled. His booted feet

squished into the brilliant red carpet as he ran after the man.

That left me alone in the room. I called Chief Michaels and briefly explained the situation. He told me to stay where I was and not let anyone touch anything.

"Don't forget you're a sworn part-time police officer, Dae," he said. "I expect you to maintain the crime scene."

I agreed to do what I could, even though I wanted to run after Mr. Lynch and the startled crew member. It was awful seeing Captain Lucky that way. I hadn't known him well, but I liked him. What had happened to him? My heart pounded as I turned away.

But I knew from being the granddaughter of a sheriff that these first moments were all important. Obviously Captain Lucky didn't drown in this room, despite the trouble someone had gone to, festooning seaweed everywhere and wetting everything down.

With shaking hands, I took a piece of seaweed from a table and put it into a disposable plastic glass from the galley area. All I could feel from it was the sea where it had grown. I bent to touch the carpet and put my finger to my tongue—there was sea water in the carpet. The big windows were closed, but someone could have shut them after the room was doused.

There were other pieces of sea life in the room. It wasn't seaweed or anything I'd ever seen before. It reminded me of a jelly fish more than anything else. I didn't touch it.

There were also orange and blue scales.

There was seaweed around Captain Lucky's neck too but no bruising. He probably hadn't been strangled.

Not that the seaweed was strong enough to strangle him.

Instead, there was a thin line of blood on the side of his head. Maybe someone had hit him and he'd fallen into the water.

But why pose him this way?

Someone had wanted him to be found. Otherwise they would have left him in the water to be dragged out to sea.

I shuddered at the idea and walked away from him again. I wasn't brave enough to touch him and possibly get the whole story. While I was curious and felt bad for him, I was also terrified what I'd see.

The ship's surgeon, a doctor from Manteo, was the next one in the room. He ran in, saw me standing next to the bed, and jumped a full foot off the wet floor.

"What are you doing in here, Mayor O'Donnell?" Doctor Gary Clark asked in a suspicious tone.

"I'm here on behalf of the town of Duck," I told him with as much authority as I could muster considering my knees were shaking. "Chief Michaels is on his way. The crime scene isn't to be disturbed."

"Well, I'm the doctor on hand, and I'm going to examine this man to make sure he's dead, if that's all right?"

"I'm sure someone professional should do that."

"Thank you."

I wasn't sure why he'd adopted that annoyed attitude with me. Maybe he was embarrassed at being caught off-guard when he came into the room. The only time I'd met him was at a party for the ship's launch. We'd barely exchanged ten words.

Dr. Clark put his hand against Captain Lucky's

throat and then looked into his eyes.

"I believe the Captain has drowned," he said. "I realize I'm not giving the official opinion. That will be up to the medical examiner. But he has all the signs of a drowning victim."

"I know it's wet in here, Dr. Clark, but not that wet. And he has a mark on his head."

"Obviously someone drowned him and then put him here." He shrugged. "We should get a sheet or something to cover him. It's disrespectful for him to be laid out this way."

Not sure what to say about that—this was my first official act at a crime scene—I got a sheet from the linen cupboard inside the walk-in closet. Even here, the sheets, towels, and all the clothing were soaking wet, dripping to the floor. I decided a wet sheet was better than none and took it out with me.

"This is wet." Dr. Clark offered to help me spread the sheet over the captain.

"Everything is soaked," I told him. "It's like this end of the ship was submerged."

"That's ridiculous," he criticized. "I'm sure there's a more rational explanation for it."

"I'm sure you're right." We finished covering Captain Lucky, and it really hit me that he was dead. Someone had taken his life. Maybe someone from Duck.

I couldn't stay in the room for another moment. I ushered Dr. Clark out and sat on a bench on deck after closing the doors behind me. That was where Chief Michaels found me about twenty minutes later. Tim Mabry, my old school friend and the man who was going to marry Trudy, was with him.

"You look weird," Tim said.

"You'd look weird too if you'd been in there." I nodded to the stateroom. Tim had always been like a brother to me, though there had been a few odd moments when we'd thought there might be something else between us. That had been a long time ago.

"Let's get this over with." Chief Michaels took a deep breath. "You know, I liked it better when we only had one or two of these every few years. Maybe we were better off not wanting Duck to grow."

"Stay here," Tim instructed me. "We'll be right out."

He didn't have to tell me to stay out of the stateroom. I picked up my phone and called Gramps. He was slightly upset because he had to reschedule his charter, but he was more upset about Captain Lucky.

"Should I close up?" he asked.

"No. Now that Chief Michaels is here, I'm sure I'll be back soon. Thanks, Gramps."

"Do you want me to call Kevin to come get you? He's not that far from where you are."

"I'll be fine. He's got a delivery and who knows what else going on. I'll talk to Chief Michaels and tell him what I know, and then I'll be back. It's okay."

Tim and Chief Michaels came out of the stateroom a few minutes later. Their faces were grim.

"Call Sheriff Riley," Chief Michaels told Tim. "Get everyone who works on this ship together so we can question them. And see if you can get a few part-time officers in to help with this."

The Town of Duck only had a police chief and two full-time officers. Basically this was all we needed for most of the year.

But we had a hundred part-time officers—including me, Kevin, and Gramps for emergencies. Our part-time officers were only paid a monthly stipend. It was the same with our fire department. Even then some folks complained about the stipend, but we all knew it was worth it for times like this when we needed the extra bodies.

"And you, young lady." Chief Michaels cornered me as Tim walked a few yards away to use his cell phone. "How did you know when to happen on these circumstances? I swear sometimes I think you must be part bloodhound."

Not sure if I should take that comparison as a compliment or not, I nodded. "Believe me, I'd rather be at Missing Pieces than here. Things happen."

He sat next to me on the bench, and we watched the frantic activity on the elaborate deck as men high above us checked the beautiful gold and red sails for the evening cruise which wouldn't take place because of Captain Lucky's death. They had surely heard the crewman's bellowing but had continued with their work.

"Why don't you start at the beginning, Dae, and tell me everything—even the weird things that I'd rather not hear."

So I started with Captain Lucky's visit to the shop and his need for money to leave town. Telling Chief Michaels the truth was different than holding back with Celia for Captain Lucky's sake. I felt bad for the captain, since everyone would know his dirty laundry and he'd have no chance to explain or make it right, but this was a murder investigation and I was the granddaughter of the former sheriff.

By the time I'd finished my story, Sheriff Tuck Riley was there listening too, his hand resting on the holstered gun at his side. Officer Scott Randall was also there to help Tim round up and question the crew of the ship. Chris Slayton, Duck's town manager, had come to offer his services as a part-time officer. With him was Cailey Fargo, the fire chief.

Duck might be small in size, but our residents all had big hearts.

When I was done, I wiped the tears from my eyes and asked Chief Michaels if I could leave. "Gramps is holding down the fort at Missing Pieces. I need to get back."

"Sure," he said. "Send him over here instead. We'll probably need his help too."

"Wait one minute, Dae," Sheriff Riley said.

The sheriff was a large, tall man with suspicious brown eyes and blond hair cut in a flat top. He had broad shoulders and a wide chest. I noticed that he'd lost a few pounds recently—probably because he was dating police Chief Heidi Palo from Corolla and wanted to look better. I was glad for both of them.

He walked with me away from the stateroom to a secluded corner of the deck.

"Anything you want to tell me?"

"I told Chief Michaels everything already," I answered. "Why are you here?"

"I'm the county sheriff, and there's been a death. I thought Ronnie could use my help."

"I see." Chalk that up for he wanted to know what was happening, and a death on the gambling ship was bound to be in the news. Tuck loved publicity. "I don't know anything more than what I told Chief Michaels."

That wasn't strictly true, as I had left out the part about the coral horn. But I didn't see how that could impact the murder investigation, and I didn't want it taken away. They might do something with it that could make this even worse.

"You know what I'm looking for." His eyebrows went up and down and his hands wiggled in the air near his face. "The spooky stuff. Woo-woo. The stuff Ronnie doesn't like to hear about."

I was surprised at the request since usually Sheriff Riley didn't want to hear anything related to my gift either.

"There wasn't anything, unless you count the death itself."

"Really? You got some vibe off it?"

"I don't know what you're looking for, but step inside the stateroom. I think you'll see what I mean."

He nodded. "Okay. If I have any questions, I'll contact you. Heidi and I have been watching all kinds of supernatural shows on TV to get a feel for what you do after everything that happened with the horses last year. I'd certainly appreciate anything you could do to help us solve this homicide."

It was such an abrupt change of attitude for him that it was hard to take in. Sheriff Riley was never a fan of my gift, and suddenly he wanted to know all about it.

"I'll be sure to let you know."

"Thanks." He enthusiastically shook my hand.

All I could think of as I went down the boarding ramp was that Heidi had made a huge difference in him.

I spoke to several other Duck residents who were

waiting to get on the ship and do their duty as part-time police officers. I was glad there were so many there that I didn't have to feel guilty about leaving.

There was no transport going from the ship to the waiting area at the end of the pier. I started walking, thinking about Captain Lucky and wondering what had happened to him. Out of the corner of my eye, I caught something large jumping in the water, close to the ship. I thought it might be a dolphin.

On the edge of the pier, the bright sunlight illuminated blue and orange scales, like the ones I'd seen in Captain Lucky's quarters. I started to pick one up with my bare hand and then drew back.

Carefully, I used my driver's license from my pocket to lift a few of the scales and put them on a piece of cardboard I found in the trash. I put that in my pocket and kept walking.

I was thinking about the coral horn and the mermaid I'd seen from touching it. Was it possible there were already seafolk in Duck?

Gramps was more than eager to go to the police investigation when I got back to Missing Pieces. He wanted to know everything I'd seen and heard at the ship, also convinced I knew something more about the crime.

"That's all I know. I hated seeing him dead. The ship surgeon said he drowned. His stateroom was wet like he could've drowned right in there. I know that's not possible."

"All right. I'm going down there. I've rescheduled the charter for tomorrow." He hugged me. "It wasn't your fault, Dae. You couldn't have known what you'd find there. I'll see you later, probably at home."

Several of the shop owners had come out on the boardwalk to talk about the gossip regarding Captain Lucky's death. It was already filtering through town.

Mary Catherine Roberts, who was the new owner of the Pet Emporium, was holding the smallest Yorkie I'd ever seen. She glanced up at the sky, and a gull landed on the edge of the gutter close to her head.

She nodded as the bird squawked a few times. "Captain Lucky has been killed? Why, that's horrible."

Vergie Smith who had been the postmistress for Duck since before I was born, paused on her way into the Duck General Store. "Hear that, August? The captain of that stupid gambling ship is dead."

August Grandin, who owned the general store, came to the open door. "I knew that ship was going to be a big mistake. Now someone's been murdered out there. I can't wait to hear what the mayor and the town council have to say about that."

Mary Catherine walked into Missing Pieces. "What's going on with Captain Lucky?" She took a seat on my burgundy brocade sofa.

"I don't know. I found him dead on the ship. I'm sure you heard as much as I know from your gull friend."

She laughed. "Gull friend. I get that. That particular gull is female too. I don't think she saw what happened to Captain Lucky, but she told me that he was here with you for a while earlier."

"Is there anything you don't hear from birds, fish, or rats?"

"Not much. They're naturally inquisitive and they love to gossip."

Mary Catherine was a colorful, middle-aged

woman who had a flamboyant sense of style—and could speak to any animal on the planet.

It was a gift, like mine, that she was born with. People called her the Pet Psychic. She'd used the name for years as a radio talk show personality. Now she was semi-retired and ran the Pet Emporium where she counseled owners and their pets when the need arose.

She'd been surprisingly busy.

Today she was wearing a green and purple caftan with matching shorts and long, faux emerald earrings. She almost always wore her large tabby cat draped around her neck like a scarf, but Baylor had been left behind, possibly because of the Yorkie she'd been holding on the boardwalk.

"I only said something about Captain Lucky's visit here to Chief Michaels. I'd appreciate it if you'd ask your friends not to spread that information around."

She laughed and walked to the door. "I don't think anyone else can understand what they say anyway, but I'll mention it to her. Now I have to go back and try to work out the problems my little Yorkie friend is having with his people."

"Maybe he just needs to eat different food," I suggested. "I took your advice about Treasure, and he's like a new cat."

"Good to hear," Mary Catherine said. "But I'm afraid the Yorkie—his name is Samuel—is far more disturbed than Treasure. He was a rescue dog, and even though he's with a good family now, he's having some lingering issues that cause him to frequently poop in the middle of his parents' bed. Not a pleasant situation. See you later, Dae."

I stood at the large plate glass window in Missing

Pieces that overlooked the boardwalk and the Currituck Sound. There were dozens of smiling tourists going in and out of the shops. It was easy to tell them apart from Duck residents that afternoon because the residents all knew about Captain Lucky's death and were either sad or angry—sometimes both—about the news.

Between customers, I took out my feather duster to run over the shelves and their contents. I checked my email, sometimes receiving offers on goods that I had listed at eBay. Nothing there, but I heard from Dillon Guthrie, a businessman I'd met. He was detailing some of the finds he'd had in South America where he was diving off the coast.

Dillon and I weren't friends. He was a thief and a killer who lived outside the law. We had nothing in common except for a deal we'd made over some valuable silver bells. I'd had one of the bells made by the Augustine monks in Florida centuries before. Dylan had given his bell to me because he thought I'd find the third bell.

And he was right. A man had offered me the third bell last month. I knew it wouldn't be long before he came to give me the details on his terms for the priceless artifact.

In the meantime, I shut off my email and paused to consider the coral horn behind the counter where I'd left it.

Captain Lucky wouldn't be coming back for it. Maybe he had a family member or friend who'd like to have it in memory of him. I wouldn't mind having my five hundred dollars back, if possible. There was no way to imagine that something like this could happen to the romantic young man who'd made such an impression on the people of Duck.

I put the horn away in the closet at the back of the shop. No doubt it was just a coincidence that Captain Lucky had been killed right after someone had sounded it.

But I didn't like those kinds of coincidences.

Chapter Four

When the shop was straightened and dusted, I was happy, and ready to bring on the huge crowds tomorrow after the parade. Sometimes I made as much in that single day as I did in a normal month. It was exciting to consider.

I had a few intriguing items that were up for sale that I had discovered over the winter.

There were two tea services that I'd found at a flea market in Morehead City. I verified their owners by touching them. They'd both belonged to the first governor of North Carolina, who by all accounts, had started his career as a pirate.

There was good evidence of the facts even before I'd removed my gloves for the rosewood tea service.

The owner claimed kinship with the governor, and my gift told me it was true. But that was only the first service.

The second service was richly appointed with gold rims and yellow jasmine flowers. That service had been owned by the governor's mistress. The rosewood had belonged to his wife. Interesting facts that I thought could help their sale price.

I also had acquired two Revolutionary War pistols and an oil lamp that was verified as being used on the Queen Anne's Revenge — Blackbeard's flagship. Usually I ignored anything attached to Blackbeard because there were so many frauds. Not to mention that discovering a piece that had been on the Revenge meant feeling all the emotions that one could imagine being on a pirate ship.

Kevin had been right beside me. I had touched the lamp gingerly. It was too valuable to ignore from my initial feelings toward it, even though he wasn't happy with me doing it. He worried a lot, but then he'd also seen me in bad straits after a few dark meetings with other artifacts.

In this case, the piece was genuine and hadn't been peppered with death and dismemberment. The oil lamp had actually belonged to the mother of a young cabin boy who'd survived Blackbeard's death at the hands of the British. He'd gone on to live a good, long life as a shoemaker in Wilmington. The lamp had been displayed in his shop until he'd passed, with him telling the story to everyone who would listen.

There was also a very fine pair of ruby and gold teardrop earrings that had been a gift from Lady Spencer while she was visiting her sister in the new world, circa 1810. It seemed that Lady Spencer had been quite well-to-do and known for dropping expensive gifts for trifles when she traveled. The earrings had been given to a housemaid who'd done a particularly good job of cleaning the lady's boots.

Besides those expensive items that would require certain customers with deep pockets, I had the usual souvenirs of the Outer Banks, a few used beach chairs, and some gently used toys. It was always good to keep some lower end stock that could prove useful to the right person.

And it was hard for me to only pick up the expensive items for my shop. I was drawn to so many things that crossed my path. Sometimes they found good homes—sometimes they lived in my shop for years.

The chime at the front door sounded. It was a young family in brightly-colored, matching cotton shorts and tank tops. They looked through everything I had and chose a few souvenirs. They asked me about the start for the parade the next day.

"We always start at nine a.m.," I told them. "We like to be done before it gets too hot."

It was the same answer I'd given many times. I was riding on a float made to look like a pirate ship this year for the first time. Everyone from town hall would be on it.

I had a few more customers, none of the caliber that would buy ruby earrings or a rare antique, but they took almost all my souvenirs and the beach chair. It wouldn't be long, and I'd have to visit local yard sales for more items to sell. I didn't like being overstocked, but I didn't like the store to look empty either.

It was getting late, and I wondered what was happening on the ship. I thought again about Captain Lucky and his dreadful death. Did Chief Michaels know what had killed him yet? I didn't want to call and ask. They didn't need my curiosity, and I'd certainly hear all about it from Gramps.

I looked at the aqua-colored dress I'd picked up for Trudy's wedding that morning. I was her maid of honor. The dress was much prettier on the hanger than it was on me, at least in my estimation. I thought it made me look like a large, unusual flower with its thick netting and calf-length skirt.

But was there ever a bridesmaid's dress that the bridesmaids liked? I'd been in dozens of weddings, and the dresses were disasters that could never be worn again. It was better than the eggplant-colored (and shaped) gown I'd worn to Althea Hinson's second wedding.

Two of the Duck town council members came to see me. I made tea for them, and we talked about what had happened to Captain Lucky.

Rick Treyburn was a retired investment banker who'd moved to Duck about ten years before. He was convinced that we were in for a rocky night at the town council meeting.

"It was bad enough that people were going to complain about too many visitors coming in for the gambling ship. Now they've got shells for their cannon."

"He's right," Councilman Dab Efird mourned. "I hope Cody Baucum has the answers. He's the most popular one."

"Everyone on the council voted for the gambling

ship," I reminded them.

"Except you, Dae," Rick said.

"I was only following the recommendations of our staff and Sheriff Riley's suggestions."

"Well it's all come to pass just like Riley and Chief Michaels said it would." Dab glared at Rick. "I felt pressured into agreeing with everyone else after the shakeup on the council."

"We'll have to come up with something," Rick agreed. "I hope you have some ideas, Dae. The new polls say that you're popular too."

We have polls? "I don't have any answers. I wish I did. We're already committed to the gambling ship. We have to find a way to make it work, even if that means hiring more police officers full-time."

Rick and Dab both drew the line at that suggestion.

"No one wants to spend extra money," Dab reminded me.

"We've been making extra money in taxes from the Andalusia," I said. "We could spend that on new officers."

"Let's get Cailey and Cody in on this too." Rick grinned. "Share the guilt. We'll see you tonight."

The town council meeting was at seven p.m. I needed to be there by six-thirty to make sure I'd seen all the information that Chris Slayton was presenting. That was part of my job as mayor, to facilitate the meetings. I rarely got to use my voting power since it only came up if there was a tie between our four council members.

It was five p.m., and though I could have stayed open later with the sunlight lasting until at least eight-thirty or nine, I had to close shop and get ready for the meeting. It hadn't been a bad day, profit wise, even though it was unlikely I would ever see the five hundred dollars back that I'd given Captain Lucky. At least I'd tried to help him.

Mary Catherine was standing at the side of the boardwalk almost leaning over the rail above the water. I walked up behind her. She was so engrossed in what she was doing, she didn't even notice me until Baylor made a sound between a meow and a cry. He was draped around her neck as usual now, almost blending in with her blond hair.

"Oh!" she said. "I'm sorry, Dae. I didn't see you there."

"That's okay." I peered over the edge of the rail too. "Just wondering what was so interesting."

There were three fish with their heads sticking out of the water. They were staring at Mary Catherine and ducked down into the sound when they saw me. Because my grandfather worked with fish, and I'd grown up on an island, I knew the fish were perch. I also knew there was good fishing off the sandbar that fronted the Duck Shoppes, though it was against the law to fish from the boardwalk.

"My friends were just telling me about a problem," she explained. "It has to do with Captain Lucky's death."

My own gifts being what they were, I never doubted what she told me.

"Did they see who killed him?"

"Not exactly. They don't live on the other side of Duck, but they have friends who do. There's something unusual about the way Captain Lucky died. It's hard to translate exactly what they're saying. You know how sometimes a fish can be garbled or misunderstand what they see. They're in the water, for the most part, and that tends to limit their view."

"What part about his death can they explain?"

"They're worried about creatures who usually don't venture up from the deepest parts of the sea. They say Captain Lucky's death has something to do with them."

I thought about the orange and blue scales I'd found on the pier and in Captain Lucky's stateroom, but I didn't mention the seafolk.

"Are we talking kraken or something?" I half joked, trying to understand.

"I'm not sure." Her forehead furrowed above her deep blue eyes. "The word they're using to describe this creature is unfamiliar to me."

I peeked through the rail at the little fish again. They seemed to be listening to what we were saying. "What's the word?" I whispered.

"*Atargatis*. Do you know it?"

"No. I don't recognize it. I guess that's the only trouble about communicating with animals."

"It's not that much different than when we find something remarkable and have to figure out what it means. I rather enjoy it." She stared off at the large expanse of water that was still colorful with kayaks and bright sailboats heading away from shore.

"Well, if you hear anything else, let me know." I smiled at her. "I have to get ready for the council meeting. I think I'm going to recommend that we never have another council meeting right before the Fourth of July parade again. I should be helping get things set up for tomorrow. Instead I'm stuck listening to people complain for two hours."

"Maybe I'll be there too," Mary Catherine said. "I know Horace is always there with Chief Michaels and Sheriff Riley."

"Since they have Captain Lucky's death to look into, none of them might be there. You should call Gramps before you put yourself through that ordeal."

"You must be headed home then." She linked her arm through mine. "I just closed too. I'll walk with you."

Walking was by far the best way to get around Duck in the summer. There could even be golf cart snarls on the roads when traffic got bad. The cool breezes blew through the stunted island trees as we followed the walking trail back to Gramps's old house.

Generations of O'Donnells had grown up here, including my grandfather and his seven siblings. Mary Catherine had come back to Duck last year and had stayed with us. She and Gramps had a thing going on, and her being there worked well for all three of us.

Knowing that Gramps had Mary Catherine was the only thing that made me feel better about moving to the Blue Whale with Kevin when we married. The two of them were a wonderful couple. I knew he wouldn't be lonely with her there. But nothing was permanent between them yet.

We reached the house and went our separate ways—Mary Catherine to my mother's old bedroom and me to mine.

Treasure, my tuxedo cat, was glad to see me. He glanced at Baylor, who was twice his size, but ignored him and went upstairs with me. Sometimes Baylor bullied Treasure a little.

My room was small but had always suited me. I was fortunate to have the entrance to the stairway from the widow's walk on the roof. From that spot, O'Donnell women had watched for their loved ones to return from the sea. I had spent many long hours gazing out at my hometown. I could see the tall masts of the Andalusia II from there, and I was always the first person to see snow on the rooftops.

I went up on the roof with Treasure for a few minutes, the two of us looking at the long line of traffic moving slowly down Duck Road. I loved the off-season months more than the long summer, despite the dip in revenue for myself and the town. I didn't like the traffic or the crowds. Duck was a peaceful corner of the world that I wished I could keep all to myself.

"If I'm going to eat anything before I face the council meeting, I'd better get a move on it," I told Treasure.

He talked back, gazing at me soulfully. I wasn't like Mary Catherine where I could understand exactly what he was saying, but I believed it had something to do with eating. I put him down when I got to my bedroom again, and he scooted out the door.

I hated to disappoint him, but I needed a quick shower and a change of clothes before I went downstairs. I was lucky that I spent so much time outside. My face was tan and needed no makeup—dark lashes, too, above my blue eyes. My hair was wild, so I kept the sun-bleached brown strands short. I could run a comb through it and be ready to go.

There was a cool, comfortable, white dress in my closet. It looked nice but didn't make me feel like I was wearing a corset. I'd set it out for tonight. A few people in Duck had complained since I'd become mayor in 2002 that I should wear a suit to meetings. I figured since they'd voted me back in for another term in office that most people didn't care if I was casual.

Duck was mostly a casual place to live. I reflected that, I decided, as the town's head officer.

There was some of my favorite pink lipstick left in the case. I put that on and practiced my wide mayor's smile in the mirror.

"Good evening, citizens of Duck. I know you've mostly come to complain, but I also know you love living here."

Of course I really wouldn't say that, but I felt like it sometimes.

The people of Duck were my friends and neighbors. Many of them still remembered my mother, Jean, and my grandmother, Eleanore. Some of them, like Trudy and Tim, I grew up with. Some of them had grown up with Gramps and could still remember when he was the sheriff.

That's the way it was, generations of hardworking Bankers who had survived hurricanes and floods and still stayed on this narrow strip of land. My kind of town.

Mary Catherine was downstairs by the time I was ready to go. She was a vision in a dark green top and matching Capri pants.

"I love your sandals," I told her. "I hope they're comfortable. Gramps has the golf cart, so we'll have to walk to town hall."

"Thank you. Not a problem walking there. I never wear anything uncomfortable. There was a time, around my third marriage, that I dressed for other people. But after my third husband passed away, I started only dressing for myself."

"A wise choice," I complimented. "I guess I've always been too interested in being comfortable to care what anyone else thought."

"You're a smart woman, Dae," she said. "Are you ready to go?"

I looked at the clock in the kitchen. It was already six-fifteen—no time for food. I'd have to eat after the meeting. "I guess we'd better leave. They look at me funny when I'm late."

The sweet twilight was coloring the sky above us with pink and orange bands that braided themselves through the blue. Headlights were starting to come on in the lines of traffic, though there was still almost two hours before dark.

We walked carefully in our summer sandals along the side of the road, mindful of a few tall weeds snagging our legs. I'd have to mention that to our public works' guys. Young men in golf carts and pickup trucks whistled and yelled at us. I ignored them, but Mary Catherine got a kick out of it and yelled back.

"It reminds me of my younger days." Her pretty face was flushed with pink. "I was quite a looker back then!"

"I think you're quite a looker right now."

"Thank you, Dae. And I appreciate you welcoming me into your family as you have. Not everyone would be so happy to see another woman with her grandfather."

"You make Gramps happy in a way I can't remember him being happy. How could I not like it?"

It hit me as we were passing the crowded Duck Shoppes parking lot that I had left a packet of information for the meeting at home. I'd been in such a last minute rush that it had completely slipped my mind.

"I have to go back home," I told her. "Maybe you could tell Nancy that I'm just running a few minutes late."

"Of course. I'll be glad to let everyone know. Are you sure you don't want me to come with you?"

"It would be better if you could keep them all calm. I should still be there before the meeting starts. Thanks, Mary Catherine."

I ran back to the house, thinking that this would be a great time for Gramps to have decided to leave the crime scene on the ship. I could make better time with the golf cart going to town hall, maybe. If nothing else, it would be easier on me.

But the drive was still empty when I got back. We'd had to start using the front door all the time until we could afford to get the back porch repaired after a February storm had damaged it.

I let myself in—we never locked the back door, but Gramps insisted on locking the front door. The key didn't want to work, but I finally got it open. Treasure was sitting on my report, cleaning himself, but paused long enough to study me and wonder why I was back so soon.

"You're sitting on my report." I slowly slid the thick file from under him. He gave me *the look*, and I knew he wasn't happy that I'd interrupted him. "Sorry. I'll see you later."

The door was even harder to lock behind me, but I

finally managed and turned to head back to Duck Road.

Someone was waiting for me. I dropped my file in the dew-kissed grass.

Chapter Five

It wasn't unusual for a resident of Duck to ask me personally for a favor or to tell me about a problem that wasn't being handled. I picked up my file and smiled.

"Sorry. I wasn't expecting anyone to be out here. I'm late for the town meeting. Maybe we could walk to town hall together and talk about your problem."

I didn't recognize the man. He was medium height and build with longish black hair that brushed his shoulders. It was getting darker. The large trees in the front yard kept the headlights on the road from identifying my caller.

"I'm sure we know each other, but this light is so bad. Have you lived in Duck long?"

"I don't live here at all," he said in halting words,

but his voice was light and beautiful.

"You must be a visitor." I held out my hand. "I'm sure you know I'm Mayor Dae O'Donnell. Someone must have pointed out my house. Everyone knows I live here, small town and everything. What's your name?"

Not wanting to waste any more time—it was six forty-five on my watch—I started resolutely back down the hill to the street, leaving him to answer as he followed me.

He paused as we walked together down the side of the road. He was jumpier than me or Mary Catherine, but not everyone was comfortable walking so close to traffic.

"Visitor," he finally said and held out his hand. "Tovi. I know who you are."

"Good. It's nice to meet you, Tovi." I flashed one of my biggest mayoral smiles at him, even though it was doubtful he got the full effect in the dusky light. "What can I do for you?"

We had just reached the far end of the Duck Shoppes' parking lot where the thick trees mostly obscured the building. It was darker here, even though there were streetlights in the parking lot.

The last buildings that had been put in had made the area darker than it was before. I hadn't been able to get the real estate company that owned the shops to add new lights.

Not yet anyway.

"What I can do for you," he said.

I could see him more clearly now, though the light didn't reach beyond his head and neck. His features were odd—aquiline nose and high cheek bones but almost no chin. He was very pale. His lips were thin and wide, almost giving him the appearance of having too many teeth in his mouth.

It bothered me looking at him. He was pretty, in the feminine sense of the word, but something about him—and the touch of his cool hand on mine—made me shiver.

"You want to do something for me?" I asked.

"Yes. I want to help you."

"What do you have in mind?" I was growing more uncomfortable by the moment.

"Your friend—the one who talks to the fish—they say you can stop bad things from happening."

We were finally in the full light of the parking lot. He was completely naked.

My voice failed for a moment as I took in his appearance. Most people would have been astonished by that since I was never at a loss for words.

I looked into his eyes. They were multi-colored. Pale blue ran with green and brown, flecks of gold in their depths. It was hard to explain, but the colors seemed to be moving, swimming.

"Who are you?" I forgot that he was naked for a moment as my heart beat fast. "How do you know Mary Catherine?"

"Come with me." He took my arm. "Let me show you."

"That's not happening." I wrenched my arm from him and started running across the crowded parking lot in a fit of panic.

I was almost run down by a fast-moving Corvette and swerved just in time to collide with another woman.

Both of us were knocked to the pavement. I got up right away to check on my victim. She was a middle-aged lady with red hair that was mostly going white. She was holding on tightly to the leash of one of the biggest dogs I'd ever seen.

"I'm so sorry." I started to help her to her feet.

But a tall man with brown hair and nice smile lines got to her first. "Are you okay, Peggy?"

"I'm fine," she said as she looked at me. "Are you all right, young lady?"

My white dress was dirty, but other than that I was unhurt. Just badly embarrassed.

"I never go running out that way," I tried to explain. "There was a man over there. He followed me from my house, and he was naked."

Peggy laughed. "This is my first visit to Duck. Does that happen often?"

"Not at all." I stuck out my hand and smiled. "I'm Mayor Dae O'Donnell. I hope you won't let this ruin your visit here. Normally we're a very peaceful town where everyone wears clothes, at least bathing suits."

She transferred the large dog's leash to her opposite hand. "I'm Peggy Lee. This is my husband, Steve, and my dog, Shakespeare. We're staying with some friends. This is such a beautiful place, and I love the rich history."

Steve shook my hand too. "Are you sure you're all right?"

"I'm fine. But very late. The town council decided to hold a meeting tonight, even though our festivities are tomorrow. We'll get through it, but I really have to go."

"Let us walk with you to town hall," Steve

suggested. "I don't see anyone naked out here right now, but he might be lurking somewhere waiting to catch you alone again."

"That's a good idea," Peggy agreed. "Steve is with the FBI, but I promise not to let him get in his investigative mood. We're on vacation, after all."

"Thank you. I appreciate your concern. Town hall is just right this way. Don't feel as though you have to stay for the meeting. It's boring for me most of the time, and I live here."

Peggy and Steve laughed, and we walked quickly through the rest of the parking lot.

"Shakespeare is a very well-trained dog," I told Peggy. "Is that what you do, train dogs?"

Steve laughed from behind us.

"Ignore him." Peggy gave him a dirty look. "Shakespeare has his moments. But no, I own a garden shop in Charlotte and I'm a part-time forensic botanist on the side."

"That's great. We have something in common. Actually we have two things in common—my fiancé is a former FBI agent, and I own a thrift store on the boardwalk. You'll have to come visit me."

"I'd love that. What's the shop's name?"

"Missing Pieces." I explained about my gift for finding lost things, and how I'd come to open the shop.

"Amazing," Peggy said. "I'd like to see you find something for someone."

I felt strange, as though I were bragging about my gift. I was saved from feeling even weirder because we'd reached the door to the room where town hall meetings were held.

To my surprise, Mary Catherine was anxiously

waiting for me.

"Are you all right?" She looked at my dirty dress. "Did you decide to work in the garden on the way?"

"I don't have time to explain now." I glanced at my watch. It was six fifty-five. Nancy Boidyn, our town clerk, was standing by my seat on the dais waving papers at me. "I have to go. It was so nice of you to walk with me. I hope we see each other again, Peggy."

Mary Catherine was touching the Great Dane and smiling at him like he was an old friend. "Is that who I think it is? Shakespeare? You're the dog that was afraid of ghosts in your new house after you were rescued."

Peggy shook her head. "Mary Catherine Roberts? You're the pet psychic. You helped me with him years ago. I always wanted to thank you but didn't know where you'd gone."

I left them shaking hands and exchanging pleasantries. It appeared that they'd met before. I wanted to stay, but the meeting had to come first. It was a packed house, as always. Our usual problem residents were right up front with their questions and suggestions. It was going to be a long night.

"You made it just in time." Chris Slayton handed me a pile of papers.

"What in the world happened to you?" Nancy tried to brush some of the trash off my back side where I'd fallen in the parking lot. There was no good way to take care of the problem.

"I'll tell you later." I took my seat behind the large, horseshoe-shaped meeting table.

"Lucky you get to sit back there." Nancy went to her desk where she recorded the meetings to be transcribed later for the archives.

"I know. How does my face and hair look?"

"You look great." Chris assured me with a smile.

"Thanks." I hadn't meant to address the question to him, but that was okay.

I put on the last bit of pink lipstick that had stayed in my pocket through everything and faced the audience as I used my gavel to call the meeting to order.

We were going through the notes from the last meeting when Sheriff Riley, Gramps, Chief Michaels, and Kevin walked into the room. One of Sheriff Riley's deputies had saved seats for them close to the front.

Chief Michaels nodded to me, which was his way of saying that he wanted to speak at a different part of the meeting than his usual police report. I nodded back in acknowledgement as Nancy finished reading the minutes.

"The minutes have been heard," I said. "Do I have a vote to approve them?"

"Aye," Rick Treyburn, Dab Efird, Cody Baucum, and Cailey Fargo all replied to the question.

"I'm Mayor Dae O'Donnell, and it's my pleasure to welcome all of you to our monthly Duck town council meeting." I smiled at the crowd before me, not happy to see Mad Dog Wilson and his friends. Next to them was our town crank, Martha Segall, who could always find something to complain about.

"Proceed with old business, Mr. Slayton," I said to Chris.

"Thank you, Mayor O'Donnell. At this time, because of the recent tragedy, I yield the floor to our police chief, Ronnie Michaels."

"I'd like to extend my condolences to the family of

Captain Bill Lucky," Cody squeezed in.

The other council members agreed.

Chief Michaels took the floor. He looked tired and more than a little upset by what had happened that day.

"I'd like to tell you that we have good news about Captain Lucky's killer, but we're still not sure what happened to him. The investigation will continue until we have answers."

"People in Duck don't feel safe here anymore." Martha spoke out of turn. "I have a petition signed by more than three thousand people who testify to that fact."

"Martha, there are only five hundred and eighty-six residents who would be eligible to sign that kind of petition," Cailey told her. "The rest of those people don't live here."

"Maybe not." Mad Dog championed her cause, heaving his large form out of his chair. "But it's not good for business if people are afraid."

Cody shook his head and covered his microphone with his hand to whisper something to Rick.

"We're doing the best we can," Chief Michaels told him. "A murder investigation takes time if it's done right."

"Just let Dae put her hands on the dead man, and we'll all know what happened," Mrs. Euly Stanley, an elderly Duck resident, remarked from the audience. "No investigation needed."

My face got hot and probably red when many people who weren't from Duck turned to stare at me. I banged my gavel once for order. "This discussion belongs in public comment, ladies and gentlemen.

Right now, Mr. Slayton has yielded the floor to Chief Michaels."

Mad Dog sat down with a disgusted grunt. Martha patted his hand.

"There's not really much more to say, Mayor," Chief Michaels reiterated. "The circumstances of the death on the ship are mysterious. Sheriff Riley will be here helping me figure them out. I'm sure the town will issue a press release if there is a breakthrough. Thank you for your time."

Chris Slayton took the floor again to proceed with old business. His report on the continuing project to build more ramps, and even an overpass for walkers to cross Duck Road, was thorough. The town had received a grant from the state for the project, which was entering its final phase.

"Work is also proceeding on the new fishing pier," Chris said. "We hope to have that completed by September."

"Are there any questions for Mr. Slayton from the council?" I asked.

"I have a question," Mad Dog shouted. "If we can build all these ramps and piers, why do we need that gambling ship? We've got plenty of tax revenue from the beach houses and businesses. I used to be on the council, you know. I know how much money we take in every year, and how much we put out. Get rid of that damn nuisance."

"Here, here!" Martha joined him.

"That ship has brought in more problems than answers," Mac Sweeney, my next door neighbor, joined the fray. "I agree with Mad Dog. I can hardly even get into the laundromat to wash my clothes."

"You're just complaining to hear yourself complain." Carter Hatley, from the skeet ball and video game arcade, Game World, got to his feet. "The Andalusia has been good for business, even in the off season."

"I agree with Carter." Mark Samson, who owned the Rib Shack, stood.

I used my gavel again to bring order to the always opinionated crowd.

"We haven't reached the public comment part of the meeting yet," I told everyone. "You'll all get your chance to speak. But for now, the next person who speaks out of turn will be asked to leave the meeting."

That had never happened at a Duck town meeting, but there was always a first time. Our meetings tended to be raucous. There weren't many of us who lived here as permanent residents, but we all had something to say. That was good — the way democracy was supposed to work. Just sometimes it got out of hand.

"That's all I have for old business," Chris said. "Shall we move on to new business?"

"Yes, please, Mr. Slayton," I encouraged. "Public comment will be after new business, for those of you who have forgotten how we hold our meetings."

Mad Dog glared at me. He knew I was talking to him after his reference to having been on the council for many years. I didn't care. He knew how this was supposed to happen.

"We don't have much in new business, Mayor O'Donnell," Chris said. "The gambling ship has been bringing in record profits for our businesses. In June, we had full occupancy of our bed and breakfast facilities as well as our vacation rental units. There is some talk of a hotel chain coming to ask about building a multi-room facility. I'm not at liberty to disclose negotiations as yet, but we should hear something about that soon."

"That's it!" Mad Dog lumbered to his feet again, his face red and angry. "Isn't this why we incorporated in the first place? We can't allow some big company to come in here and ruin Duck."

Chief Michaels shot to his feet in the back of the room. "For the love of God, Randal, sit down and shut up. We have enough real problems without you causing more."

It was so uncharacteristic of Chief Michaels to speak that way—the room grew instantly silent. He gazed at all his friends and neighbors and then started to speak again. His face turned a ghastly shade of gray and he gripped his chest with his hands.

As we all watched, Chief Michaels collapsed on the council room floor.

"Somebody call an ambulance!" Carter Hatley yelled.

Chapter Six

It took thirty minutes for an ambulance to reach us from Kill Devil Hills.

In the meantime, Kevin went to get Dr. Clark who was still at the ship waiting for a morgue pickup. They got back faster than I imagined possible while Sheriff Riley and Tim did CPR on Chief Michaels.

Dr. Clark stabilized Chief Michaels as Chris and Nancy moved people out of the meeting room. Even Mad Dog and Martha were quiet during that time.

I stayed in the room with Chief Michaels's wife, Marjory, and his sister, Ladonna. We held hands as the paramedics arrived to take him to the hospital.

"I should go with him," Marjory said.

"We'll be right behind you," I promised. "I'll bring

Ladonna with me."

There were several vehicles following the ambulance to the hospital, including two police cars escorting it to make sure traffic stayed out of the way. We didn't stop for red lights, although several cars honked their horns as we went by.

At the hospital, the waiting room was full of Duck residents, anxious for word of Chief Michaels.

Kevin brought coffee from the Blue Whale in large urns. We were all grateful for the hot beverage. There was nothing to be done about the uncomfortable, hard plastic chairs, although Chris Slayton managed to fall asleep in one. Everyone else sat and stared at each other or at the TV on the wall.

At ten p.m., Cailey Fargo called me in to a small family meeting room where Rick Treyburn and Dab Efird were already seated. Cody Baucum came in right after. Nancy was there with a pen and paper. I knew what this was about.

"I know it's sudden," Cailey said, "but we have to consider what to do about an immediate replacement for Chief Michaels."

"Replacement?" The word sounded torn from Dab's throat. He and Chief Michaels were very close. "We don't know how bad this is. We don't have to replace the man already."

Cailey shook her head. "I don't mean a permanent replacement, but we're shorthanded enough for the busy season. We need someone to temporarily take up the reins of the police department. When Ronnie is ready to come back, that's fine. We just can't risk any more chaos in the middle of a murder investigation and twenty-thousand people in the streets for the Fourth of

July."

We all agreed, though no one was happy about the situation.

"Do you have someone in mind?" Cody asked.

"Yes. I already took the liberty of speaking with him before I brought his name up."

Rick nodded. "Horace O'Donnell, right? Nobody knows this town like he does, and he has the benefit of having been sheriff."

Maybe that had immediately occurred to Rick and Cailey, but not to me.

"Surely it would be better to promote Tim Mabry to take the chief's place and hire one or two part-time officers," I suggested. "Tim has been with the police department since it started."

I wasn't thrilled with the idea of Gramps taking on that responsibility, especially with the murder investigation and all the tourists.

"Tim is a good man," Cailey said. "But he just doesn't have the maturity to handle this."

"Agreed," Cody said. "Though I think Dae is right about creating a few more full-time officers at least until we get through this crisis."

"But Gramps is too old for this," I argued. "I don't know if it will be too much of a strain for him." I was completely rattled by my grandfather agreeing so quickly to take Chief Michaels's place, even if it was only for a few weeks.

"Horace is the same age as Chief Michaels," Cailey said.

"And Chief Michaels just had a heart attack," I reminded her.

But in the end, the police chief in Duck is appointed

by the town council. I did my duty as mayor and called for a vote on the matter, hoping there would be a tie that I would have to break. I'd vote against Gramps being police chief and suggest again that Tim should take Chief Michaels's place.

There was no tie. All four council members quietly spoke their votes to bring in Gramps as interim police chief. As soon as the vote was over, Cailey brought Gramps into the room, and the four council members shook his hand and thanked him for his service.

I couldn't bring myself to do that and walked quickly out of the meeting room.

"What's going on?" Kevin asked when he saw me.

"They want Gramps to take Chief Michaels's place," I said in a low voice. "I wish he would've turned them down."

"Why? He was good at what he did. The town needs him right now."

My eyes filled with tears that I brushed away. "I need him too. They should've tapped Tim. He could've done the job."

He put his arm around me. "He'll be okay, Dae. Don't worry. And I'm sure Ronnie Michaels isn't going to lie around in bed for very long either. It'll be fine. Have some faith, like you're always telling me."

Gramps and the council came out of the meeting room. My grandfather's gaze immediately came to rest on me across the room.

We would have discussed what we'd done at that point, but Chief Michaels's doctors came into the visitors' area at the same time.

"There's good news and bad news," the lead cardiologist said. "Chief Michaels survived a serious cardiac event. He's going to need surgery, and I'm afraid, a long recovery time."

There were many questions, but no one was surprised by the severity of the event. We were as prepared as we could be, even though I still would have argued the point about Gramps being police chief, if anyone would have listened.

We said goodnight a short time later. Gramps came home with Kevin and me in Kevin's old pickup truck. Ladonna and Marjory stayed at the hospital, but a few of us agreed on a schedule so that they could have some time away.

It was a quiet ride for the first twenty minutes with me squished between Gramps and Kevin.

I wanted to say something, probably ask him not to take Chief Michaels's place. The words just wouldn't come.

Finally, Kevin broke the silence. "I'm not letting the two of you out of this truck until I know that everything is okay between you."

Gramps chuckled. "I see a throw-down coming in your future, young man."

"That's okay," he said. "Isn't there something you want to say, Dae?"

"I don't know," I muttered.

"If you have something, spit it out," Gramps said.

"All right." I faced him. "I don't think you should do this. If I could've voted, I would've voted against it. Tim should step in. He's been there long enough to know what he's doing."

"Is this because you're afraid for me or because you think Tim deserves the promotion?" Gramps questioned.

"Both," I answered honestly. "Although I'm more worried about you getting hurt than about Tim getting a promotion. It's been a long time since you carried a badge and a gun. Things have changed."

"Things haven't changed that much," Kevin said. "Once you've done the job, you can go back to it any time."

"But you're not volunteering," I mentioned hotly.

"No, I volunteered," Gramps said. "I'll be fine, Dae. I can handle this. I'm sorry you're afraid for me, but nothing will happen."

"Tell that to Captain Lucky," I said. "It's bad enough having a murder investigation right now, but it's also prime beach season."

"I don't know what else to say." Gramps shook his head as we rolled into our driveway.

I had completely forgotten about the naked man until that moment. So much had happened so quickly. I started to say something about it, but was afraid that Gramps and Kevin would just think I was throwing more roadblocks in the way.

"It's a bad situation," I said as Kevin parked the truck. "I don't want it to get any worse."

"It won't, honey." Gramps squeezed my hand before he got out of the pickup. "I'm going inside. It's been a long day, and I have to be up early tomorrow. I'll see you later, Kevin. Thanks for the ride."

He walked slowly to the house. I watched him until he was inside and the door had closed behind him.

"This isn't right," I told Kevin. "I know there isn't anything I can do about it, but I'm really worried about him."

He took me in his arms and kissed me. "I

understand, but Horace will be fine. That's why they wanted him for the job. He knows what he's doing, and he knows this town. You have to have some confidence in him."

"I hope so. If not, you'd probably be next on the interim police chief list. All the council members feel like Tim is too young and immature. He and I are the same age. That makes me question how they feel about me too." I hugged him back and grabbed my bag. "Goodnight, Kevin. I'll see you at the parade tomorrow."

Mary Catherine wanted to hear all about it, of course, so we were up talking until well after midnight. She finally said goodnight and went up to her room, leaving Gramps and me in the kitchen.

"I hope you'll feel better about this later." He put the coffee cups into the dishwasher. "Give your grandfather a little credit here, honey. You know I'm as good as my word. Nothing is going to happen to me."

I hugged him, closing my eyes, and prayed he was right. If I lost him, all my family would be gone. "I love you, Gramps. Please be careful."

"When have I ever *not* been careful?" he asked with a twinkle in his blue eyes. "Let's get to sleep. Big day tomorrow."

I carefully took the cardboard with the gold and blue scales out of my pocket. They didn't look as impressive after being in there all day — more like dried fish scales. I got undressed and got into bed with Treasure sleeping beside me. I thought about Chief Michaels, Gramps, and the naked man I'd left behind in the Duck Shoppes parking lot.

Once in a while, a few party people came to Duck

and odd things of that nature happened. It didn't really worry me about the naked man.

And Chief Michaels would be fine, I promised myself. Gramps would be too.

But the possible threat against him made me open the drawer to my bedside table and pull out my grandmother's old watch.

I'd experimented with it before, finding that my gift for seeing people and their history behind the items I touched could extend to actually being in that past moment.

I wasn't a real person when I was there—more a ghost-like figure—but it had been a way that I could meet my grandmother who'd died before I was born. She'd warned me at one of those meetings that, while it was possible to visit with loved ones in the past, I had to be careful, or I would become trapped in that past too.

That's what had happened to her. All those years I'd thought she was dead, but instead she just never came back. I'd told Gramps about my meeting with Grandma Eleanore. He knew about the gift we shared and the consequences it could have. He'd asked me to promise him that I wouldn't do it again.

I'd agreed—at that time.

It was different now. I'd tried various objects that had belonged to her, believing that I might be able to bring her back with me to my time. Nothing had worked. Her watch was still my best anchor to her, but our visits were always the same.

The watch was pretty and lightweight. I held it in my hands and closed my eyes to feel her presence. In a thought I was there, sitting at the same kitchen table that I'd just left, only forty years earlier.

"Oh my goodness, Dae. You startled the daylights out of me," Grandma Eleanore said. "But it's good to see you again. I have news. Can you stay for tea?"

Chapter Seven

I could tell the differences in the kitchen, things that had changed since I was a child. There was an old green stove with a percolator instead of a coffeemaker on the cabinet and wood paneling on the walls instead of the wallpaper with roses that my mother had put in.

"This is a good time for you to visit." She made us both a cup of tea.

There were times when I went back that I was nothing more than a ghost and other times when it was like I was really there. I could feel, smell, and taste things. I didn't know what the difference was. This was still new to me.

"I'm so happy to be here. It's been a rough day in Duck."

"I don't know how long you'll be here so I'd better get right to the point." She put a cup of tea in front of me—fragrant jasmine.

I inhaled and closed my eyes. Grandma Eleanore was so like my mother, but my grandmother and I shared the gift that had bypassed her. If it hadn't, I might have been able to visit her too. Wanting to see my mother again was a terrible yearning that lived in my soul after she'd abruptly died one evening when her car went off one of the bridges that joined Duck to the mainland.

It had happened after we'd had a bad quarrel while I was still in college. She'd left to go home early because of an approaching storm. No one had ever seen her again.

"What is it?" This place in time had become a haven for me. I didn't like the idea that something could upset it.

"I believe I figured out a way for you to come back and visit with your mother."

"How?"

"You know that you have to hold something that connects you to that person and the time." She sat opposite me. "You've come back at times when you've seen your mother, but she can't see you because she doesn't have our gift."

"Yes, I know that. What can make that different?" I was impatient for the answer because I knew she was right and the connection between us could be broken at any moment.

"There was a traveling psychic who came to town last week for a carnival. I believe he was the real thing. I spoke with him briefly, just to get a feel for him. Dae, if you came back at the moment when your mother met with him, I think he could bridge the gap between you. You could speak with her through him."

I was amazed at the idea. "That would mean I could warn her not to go home the night that she died. She could still be alive in my time. You're a genius, Grandma Eleanore!"

"You can't do that. I just meant you could talk to her. You can't try to change her fate. You don't know what else will change if you do that."

"I don't care. Do you know how awful my life has been since the last thing we said to each other was in anger? I've had dreams since that day of her sitting in her car underwater, waiting for me to find her. I could stop all that."

"At what risk? What are you willing to give up? It could be that your grandfather will be dead instead of your mother. It could be that she'd be alive but in a coma or crippled. We can go back in the past, darling, but we can't change it."

"Is that why you're trapped in the past? I've tried my best to find that moment when we lost you, but I don't have a lot of your possessions. What should I use to contact you during that time and bring you back?"

"You can't bring me back either." She smiled gently. "I wish you could. But even if I knew what possession you could use, I wouldn't tell you. You can't change things that happened before you were born. I made that mistake. Don't you make it too."

"How do you know that's what trapped you in the past?"

"Let's not waste our time on things we can't do," she said. "Your mother won a stuffed unicorn with a rainbow horn. I don't know for sure that she kept it as an adult, but she was a great believer in saving everything. If you can find it, use it to contact her through the psychic. Be careful what you say. I love you, Dae."

"Grandma—"

"You're starting to fade. Tell your grandfather that I love him. Goodbye, darling."

I came back to myself in my time, breathing as hard as if I'd run a marathon. My heart was pumping fast. I had a difficult time separating myself from the past.

Treasure softly cried out in his sleep and snuggled closer.

I was still in my bed, still clutching Grandma's old watch. I realized that I was crying. I wanted to bring her back and find a way to talk to my mother. Sometimes it was all I could think about.

For years, I'd gone to séances with my friend, Shayla, as she attempted to contact my mother. None of them had worked. But maybe Grandma Eleanore was right and the traveling psychic could work as a conduit between me and my mother.

Shayla had moved back to her home in New Orleans. I had given up séances when I realized, by accident, that I could travel into the past holding an object that came from that time. I'd thought it was the way to be with my mother again.

Even though it was barely two a.m., I got up and went up to the attic to look for the rainbow unicorn. If there was a chance, I'd be willing to take it.

Gramps found me there two hours later. "What in the world are you doing up here? Have you been up all night?"

"I've been looking for something that belonged to Mom. A rainbow unicorn she got from a carnival when she was a kid. There was a psychic. Sound familiar? Do you have any idea where that could be?"

"I'm sorry, Dae. I don't know what you mean." He surveyed the crowded attic, most of which consisted of tumbled boxes, old clothes, and toys.

I told him about my visit with Grandma Eleanore.

He wasn't happy about it. "I thought you said she told you it was dangerous to go into the past."

"I don't care. I have a chance to warn Mom about the day she died. How can I let that go?"

Gramps frowned. "I don't know what to say, honey. But right now I have to get to work, and you have to go over to town hall to get everything set up. You have the parade schedule. If you aren't there to get the cars and floats lined up, who will?"

Reluctantly, I agreed with him. I noticed he was wearing the dark blue Duck police officer's uniform. It made him look completely different, more like when I was a child and he was the sheriff.

"You look nice," I told him. "Be careful out there today. Do you have any idea who you're going to tap to be temporary police officers?"

"Cody volunteered. Reece wanted to as well, but they couldn't both be away from the restaurant for full shifts. Mark Samson's daughter, Diane, offered to help out. And Dale Fargo said he'd give us a hand. He's only working part-time at the gambling ship."

"You sure got them signed up fast since last night."

"Email. And I don't mess around when I have a promise to keep."

"To Chief Michaels?"

He hugged me and whispered, "To my granddaughter. I promised her I'd stay safe."

"I love you. Grandma Eleanore said to tell you that she loves you too."

Gramps let me go as he looked away. "About that, Dae. I have a good thing going with Mary Catherine right now. She and I have a lot in common, and I think I might be in love with her."

That didn't really surprise me. I could tell they were attached to each other because they were so happy together.

"I know. It's okay. You both deserve to be happy."

"The thing is, honey, I can't keep thinking about your grandmother and let myself feel anything for MC. It feels like I'm cheating on Eleanore when I kiss her."

That was depressing. "So you don't want me to try to bring her back?"

He rubbed his hand over his freshly shaved face. "I don't know what to think about it. Do you think I should push MC away until we figure out if your grandmother is coming back?"

"No. Of course not. Grandma Eleanore says she can't come back, not without some catastrophic event happening. Mom either." I sighed and felt like crying. "I guess we go on without them."

He rubbed my arm. "I don't know what else to do but move forward. You're the only one left of my family. I've had to put a lot of loss behind me. The only way I know to do that is to keep making fresh starts."

"I understand. I won't bring it up again."

"I don't mean that like it sounds," he amended. "I'll always love Eleanore, but in a different way than I love MC right now. I suppose that's hard for you. I'm sorry."

"I understand." I kissed his cheek. "You'd better get going so you can summon the troops. Any word on Chief Michaels?"

"Actually, I was already there this morning. He's still isn't awake from his surgery, but the doctor said everything went well. Agnes Caudle and Betty Vasquez are down there now so Ladonna and Marjory can get some rest."

"That's good news. I guess I'll see you later."

"Are you sure you're okay?"

"I'm fine. I hope you get to see some of the parade."

After he went downstairs, I went back to my room and got dressed.

Gramps's relationship with Mary Catherine wasn't something I'd thought about in my quest to bring Grandma Eleanore home. I supposed it would be awkward for them, but surely it was worth it too. I didn't want to think about how it would affect everyone. If there was some way to get her back from where she was trapped in the past, I knew I'd do it and then deal with the fallout later.

Despite Grandma Eleanore's warnings, I felt the same way about my mother. Maybe I couldn't bring her back, but I could warn her through the psychic. She'd know not to go home the day she died. I couldn't see where that could hurt anything.

But as much as I wanted to find the rainbow unicorn and warn her, I had to deal with the Fourth of July first. It was right here, right now. Everything else would have to be on hold until it was over.

I smiled as I dressed, thinking that time was a

relative thing to me anyway. I had gone back forty years to see my grandmother last night. I'd gone back further in other visits when I'd touched objects from the past.

My white shorts were a little shorter than I usually wore them, but with the heavy wool Mayor's coat I'd have to wear over them, I thought they'd be comfortable. I wore my shorts with a patriotic red, white, and blue-striped tank top. Both items looked good with my early summer tan.

My slimmed-down version of the Duck mayor's coat was waiting for me at my office in town hall, according to a text I'd received from Darcy. She was our local dressmaker who'd also made Trudy's wedding gown and bridesmaid dresses. I couldn't wait to see the coat. I hoped it fit me better than the last time I'd worn it.

I put on some lip gloss and sunblock and then slipped my feet into tennis shoes for the running I'd be doing that day. My phone promised clear skies and mild temperatures, at least for the morning during the parade. I left Mary Catherine a note telling her where Gramps and I had gone and then skipped out of the house with my parade clipboard in hand.

It was still dark, and Duck Road was quiet. The air was misty and cool with the milky crescent moon floating in the sky above me. I was looking forward to the parade and even the hectic part of the day.

The parade route was starting at town hall this year. We had a huge parking lot for staging the event. It had always started at the Duck Shoppes. Because it meant not having customers in and out during the two hours of the parade, the real estate company that owned the shops had never been happy about it.

I had never understood their complaints since traffic was stopped on Duck Road for that time and cars couldn't get through anyway.

It didn't matter anymore, I thought, as I passed the coffeehouse and bookstore, the only lighted building in the area. The new town hall had been wonderful for many different reasons. And soon the footbridge that would go over Duck Road would be finished too. Chris Slayton was a wizard when it came to great ideas—and money to get them accomplished.

I heard a sound to the right of me in the grassy area next to the coffeehouse where Chris's wife, Jamie, would be up getting things ready for the day. As I turned my head to see what was going on, someone wrapped their arms around my midsection, lifted me, and began moving very quickly toward the sound.

Chapter Eight

For a moment, I was so surprised that I didn't move or resist. That's how long it took me to realize that this shouldn't be happening.

Once I understood the situation, I began kicking and beating at the person who was holding me. I tried to find eyes to gouge and skin to scratch, but I kept missing. I was amazed at how fast we were moving. I'd seen the firefighters training—they never moved this fast.

But they probably weren't as strong as this man either. I could feel it in the careless way he held me. There was no strain at all.

"Let me go!" I yelled and finally started screaming for help.

"Quiet, please." The voice was familiar and didn't seem angry that I was trying to hurt him.

"Put me down. If you have something to say, I can listen on my feet. You don't have to carry me away."

"I won't hurt you. We're almost there."

I realized when he spoke again that it was the naked man from last night. I should have talked to someone about him.

Too late now.

His shoulders was cool and clammy under my hands. They had a spongy consistency that was unusual for normal skin. I couldn't stop myself from questioning—merman? Was that possible?

He ran up the ramp to the boardwalk. His muscles bunched tightly together just before he jumped across the rail and landed on the sandbar adjacent to the shops.

History said that this had been a popular place for parties back in the 1930s. The historical society had dug up dozens of old whiskey bottles and other artifacts. But why come here?

My heart pounded as I renewed my efforts to escape.

The man, who held me like a baby in his arms, abruptly set me down on my feet. I could feel the water and sand ooze into my tennis shoes. The light from the crescent moon shone on his face. The shops were quiet and dark behind him.

"Why are you doing this?" I felt more secure since I was standing. I glanced around for a weapon of some sort. There was a broken wooden oar beside me on the sand, but it didn't look like much.

"You must hear what I have to say. I know you are

the ruler of this place. I am here to help you."

"Ruler? I'm the mayor, if that's what you mean." Was this just some weird way of complaining about something he didn't like? I was sure I had never seen him before—except for last night. He was still naked, and a little greenish in the moonlight.

Merman, my mind whispered.

Shut up!

"Yes. Whatever your term is for your authority. I am Tovi. I have come on behalf of the sea folk to tell you that we are not responsible for the death of your ship captain."

I was mesmerized by his strangely moving eyes as they shifted from green to blue to brown. How could anyone's eyes move that way? They looked like an old lava lamp, sending gold sparks through the colors. He was so strange, and yet so beautiful. His accent was strange too. Where was he from?

Under the sea, my imagination replied. *Travis called him with the horn.*

Shaking off the fascination, I tried to set him straight. "Look. I'm the mayor. That's true. But I think you need to talk to the police. I'm not in charge of people dying, and if you know something about Captain Lucky's death, you should report it. But not to me."

"Are you listening to what I say?" he asked in an impatient tone. "I only have a short while remaining this day before I must go. I have lived centuries, and I know the ways of man. I know of your captain's death, but I wasn't the cause of it. Do not look for me. Only war between us can ensue if they hunt for us."

Not really sure if I should laugh at him—he might

be more than a little disturbed—I tried to keep a straight face when I spoke. "Captain Lucky's death is tragic, but I don't think anyone is going to war over it. Are you from around here?"

He shook me. It wasn't hard, more like you'd shake someone to wake them up.

"Are you listening to me, woman? Or are you insane?"

Funny, since I'd been partially thinking that about him. The other part that made my skin creep and my brain race was thinking that he was a merman.

"I really think you should come with me to talk with our police chief. It will only take a few minutes." I carefully enunciated every word, hoping he would understand.

He glanced sharply at the horizon. "The sun is coming. Meet me here at sundown. We can speak with your police chief then. But mind you, do not try to follow me. This could mean your death."

Inside, I was thinking, *you don't have to worry about it.* I could always send Tim or Scott after him. Outside, I just maintained my composure and nodded that I understood.

"Good. I go to my rest."

As soon as he'd said the words, he slipped into the water. There was no splash. He didn't dive or fall in. It was almost as though he melted into the Currituck Sound and merged with it.

I caught my breath as there was no other movement. I waited a few minutes. He didn't re-surface from the gray water.

Merman! I knew it!

"Tovi?" Should I jump in after him? He could have

just committed suicide if I was wrong about him. "Tovi?"

Quickly, I took off my shoes and grabbed the life preserver that was always hanging from the rail on the boardwalk. I stepped into the water on the edge of the sandbar and would have dived in after him, but just as suddenly, his head surfaced.

"What are you doing? I told you not to come after me."

"I can't let you kill yourself. Come back up here. Let's talk about it. I'm sorry if I didn't listen carefully enough. It's okay. I believe you about Captain Lucky. I'm sure someone else killed him."

He smiled at me slowly. "You are one of the good humans, aren't you? I thought as much when I spoke with you. My people praise me for having an understanding of the land dwellers."

"I like to think that I'm a good person. Now, please come out of the water. We can go to my shop, right there on the boardwalk." I pointed to Missing Pieces. "I'll make you some tea, and we can talk."

"I cannot return to the land at this moment. But I will be back tonight at sundown. Please meet me there, and we shall drink tea."

"Okay. Just come up out of the water. Please. I don't want you to drown."

He laughed at me. "At sundown. Farewell until then."

He ducked his head again below the water, but this time there was a splash as a large, blue, gold, and orange tail flipped straight up in the water and then sank beneath it. The movement threw water on me. I put up my hands uselessly to try to keep my outfit dry.

As I kept watching, I saw his head again followed by the movement of the tail as he dove underwater.

"No one is ever gonna believe this." I sat right down on the wet sandbar, my legs giving out from under me as I realized what I'd seen.

A merperson. Merman. Seafolk, he'd called his people.

I remembered Captain Lucky saying the coral horn could call the seafolk. After that moment, I began to give credence to what Tovi had said. I tried to recall every word and dissected it over and over again in my mind.

There were really people who lived in the water. All the legends were true. I was excited and frightened. I couldn't tell anyone. They'd all think I'd lost my last hold on reality.

My shoes squished, and my butt was wet as I forced myself to get up and walked down the quiet street to town hall. I wanted to shout to the town that I'd met a merman. I wanted everyone to know.

But what proof did I have?

There were dozens of people at town hall already, working on the big pirate ship float that was being built on the back of Mad Dog's flatbed truck. I'd been surprised that he'd volunteered to let us use it—until I found out that he'd traded Chris Slayton the use of the truck for a ride in the parade.

I didn't blame Chris for accepting, and I didn't care if Mad Dog still thought of himself as being on the town council. He wasn't—that was all that mattered.

"You're squishing, Dae," Nancy said as the early morning breeze blew her straight, reddish brown hair into her blue eyes. "Take a shower and forget to take off your shoes?"

I met a merman!

"No. I was splashed by a truck that went by on Duck Road as I was walking here."

She looked into my face intently. "Are you okay? You look kind of strange. And you might want to rethink that story since there haven't been any puddles on the road in weeks."

I thanked her and moved away to speak with Chris and Jamie Slayton. Nancy sometimes knew me too well. Not that my story wasn't a little crazy sounding. I'd been so busy thinking about people living in the water that I hadn't thought of a good reason that I was wet and sandy.

"Morning, Dae," Chris said. "The weather report is sunny, ninety degrees, and dry for this morning. Good news, huh?" He put another piece of black tissue paper on the hull of the pirate ship float.

"Very good news," I agreed as I put tissue paper on the float too.

I wanted to ask him and Jamie what they thought about mermaids and mermen, but I couldn't talk about it yet. There had to be some intelligent way to get the subject out in the open.

"I could smell the bread baking at the Blue Whale this morning while I was walking up here," Jamie said. "I've been starving ever since. I'm sorry Kevin couldn't be here to help out with the parade. He was really good at organizing everything last year."

"Dae will be good at it too," Chris said. "Are your shoes wet?"

I thought of another excuse for why my tennis shoes were squishing—a better excuse than I'd given

Nancy. "My dryer is broken."

We continued working on the last minute touches for the pirate ship as more floats, trucks, and convertibles lined up in the parking lot. I wished I could talk to Kevin about what had happened with Tovi, but there just wasn't time. Even though the parade wasn't until nine, there was so much to do.

I grabbed my clipboard and the official Duck Mayor's coat from my office in the town hall building. I set aside the wet tennis shoes—I always kept an extra pair of comfortable but worn sandals there. I wasn't walking down Duck Road in the parade this year, so I thought they'd make it through the event. Once the parade was over, I could go home and grab another pair of shoes.

When the clear plastic was stripped from the mayor's coat, I saw the smiley face sticker that Darcy had left on the lapel. I tried the coat on right away. She'd done a wonderful job making it smaller and lighter. There were spots where she'd replaced the heavy wool with a lighter fabric in the sides and under the sleeves where no one would notice. She'd left the red sashes, ribbons, and gold coins that edged the neck, but the sleeves ended before my wrists.

It was a much better fit. I hoped the next person to wear it wouldn't have to let it out, but if they did, Darcy could probably fix it for them too.

I closed the door to the office and looked in the full-length mirror on the back of it. The coat was still going to be hot for a day in the nineties, but if that was part of being mayor, I was glad to do it.

Had I really seen a merman on the sandbar? It seemed real enough, and goodness knew I had seen many other strange things. It was going to be hard keeping it to myself until I could tell Gramps, Kevin, or maybe Mary Catherine. Otherwise I was looking forward to the day and anticipating my visitor at sundown.

Under flawless blue morning skies, the biggest crowd ever—at least according to my estimates—stood and cheered the parade as it went by them on Duck Road.

There were a few floats—none as imaginative or grand as the town hall float. Dozens of boats on trailers were decorated with red, white, and blue streamers and pulled down the road with occupants waving. One police car with sirens wailing and lights flashing came through to remind people that Duck had a police department. Both fire engines and a squad of paramedics from Kill Devil Hills also joined the fun.

The Duck Historical Museum members walked through the streets dressed like pirates. Mrs. Euly Stanley wore the same colonial era dress she always wore. Vergie Smith from the post office strolled with her, wearing a lovely periwinkle gown.

Mike's Surf Shop was represented by several area surfers wearing their darkest tans and very little else as they carried their surf boards and waved. Andy Martin gave out tiny ice cream cones to everyone, and Walter Perry, who owned Duck Donuts, gave out free samples of his pastries.

Miss Duck rode by in her boyfriend's red convertible. Misses Manteo and Corolla joined her in the backseat. Miss Outer Banks rode in her own black convertible wearing a revealing swimsuit that every man cheered as she went by.

We'd asked Miss North Carolina to join us as well, but she couldn't make it. We did get the Azalea Queen from Wilmington to be there along with the Honey Bee Queen from Albemarle. She even brought her princess bees.

Of course, there were marching bands from the local high schools and a few gymnastic classes whose participants did cartwheels and other acrobatic feats along the parade route. There were cloggers and square dance clubs that danced their way down Duck Road.

Mayor Lisa Fitz and Chief Heidi Palo from Corolla waved from their shared SUV as they tossed candy to the kids in the crowd.

It was a wonderful Fourth of July parade. Chris Slayton gave out flyers to remind everyone that there would be fireworks at Duck Municipal Park that night. Everyone was laughing as the parade finished. They were looking for something to drink, snacks, and places to shop.

At least I hoped they were looking for fun things to buy at *my* shop.

The parade ended at the fire department. Once all the vehicles had reached that destination, they were free to travel back on Duck Road. Walkers dispersed right away, some running back up the road to the Duck Shoppes.

"A wonderful parade!" Cathi Connor, principle of Duck Elementary School, said with a smile. She'd been with the Historical Museum group and was dressed as a mermaid with a long blond wig, and a gold tail she held up using a string tied to her left hand so she could walk.

Cathi and I had grown up together, friends through

high school. She'd been married for a while and had left Duck but had come back a few years ago.

"How do you like my costume?" She pirouetted around me so I could appreciate what she was wearing.

"Is a mermaid considered historical?" I asked, desperately wanting to tell her about the merman.

"I think so. Yes. They aren't around today, like pirates. But I think there were some mermaid sightings around Duck. We have plenty of firsthand accounts and drawings at the museum. You know, even Christopher Columbus claimed to have seen a mermaid."

"If it's good enough for Chris Columbus, I guess it's good enough for me."

"Darn straight." Cathi grabbed my arm, and we walked away from the main group of revelers. "I can't believe Captain Lucky was killed. I wasn't surprised that you found him since you have a nose for that type of thing. Who do you think did it?"

"Yes, Mayor O'Donnell." The owner of the new Duck newspaper, *Duck Aloud*, pushed his way into our conversation. "Why don't you tell us all about it?"

Chapter Nine

Manfred Vorst was the editor-in-chief and owner of the newspaper. He was a pale little man considering he lived in a warm climate. His red hair was thinning, but he spiked it up to make it look like he had more. He had a sharp nose and blue eyes behind thick glasses. His newspaper had only been running for about six months, but it was popular because his cartoons made fun of city officials.

I'd been featured several times with my gavel in hand and a crown on my head. He wasn't exactly my favorite person, though I was happy to have a newspaper in town again. I wished many times it was more a real newspaper than a gossip rag.

"There's not much to tell," I said. "I went to the ship to return something Captain Lucky had dropped at my shop, and I found him dead in his stateroom."

"I heard that he had drowned," Manfred said. "He was just posed in his room but died elsewhere. Is that also true?"

"I don't know all the details," I denied. "You'd better talk to the police chief."

"It sounds like you and Sir Horace will be running the whole town soon." Manfred rocked back on his heels and sneered at me. "Once you marry Kevin Brickman, the show will be all in the family."

"Excuse me." I walked away from him but heard him questioning Cathi about our relationship.

Since I really wanted to talk to Kevin, I headed for the Blue Whale instead of Missing Pieces. The mayor's coat was steamy.

Gramps went by in a police car. It was so odd seeing him in that capacity again. I waved, but he looked too deep in thought to notice me. I wondered if there was any new information about Captain Lucky's death.

Which brought me back to thinking about seafolk.

I wasn't sure why Tovi thought we'd even consider that someone who lived under water would have killed Captain Lucky. I supposed he didn't realize that most people in Duck probably didn't believe mermaids existed. They were fast to believe in pirate curses and ghosts, but I'd never met anyone talking about seafolk in casual conversation.

For all his boasting about understanding humans, Tovi didn't know as much about us as we knew about him.

Cars and golf carts were hard pressed to get down any roads in Duck due to heavy pedestrian traffic. I walked on the side of the road, but almost everyone else walked right down the middle. There were so many strangers that I only saw a few familiar faces. I saw Althea Hinson, who was a librarian in Manteo, and Molly Black from the Curbside Bar and Grill.

"Thank goodness Kevin keeps extras on hand." Molly smiled as she hurried by me. "The day has barely started, and we're out of butter. Can you imagine? See you later, Dae."

I reached the Blue Whale, which was also crowded since Kevin was holding open house all day. The double front doors were exposed to the strong breezes coming from the Atlantic. There was a wide circle drive in front of the inn with a large fountain in the middle green space. A mermaid smiled flirtatiously from her watery home as I walked by.

Kevin had left the hitching post at the front of the building to keep the original feel to the old place. Dozens of visitors were sitting on the rocking chairs that graced the verandah, cold drinks in hand.

I went quickly past them and headed to the kitchen where I knew Kevin would be. He had hired six high school students to walk around the inn and grounds giving out food samples and making sure everyone was happy. From what I could see, the idea was a huge success. I liked the inn better when it wasn't so crowded that I could hardly move, but I was glad business was good.

Kevin was in the kitchen with a staff of three cooks. They were getting ready for lunch that would be served in the big dining room to the back of the building, as well as on the verandah and in the back garden. The wonderful aromas, as Jamie had mentioned, were enough to make my stomach rumble.

"Dae! I thought you'd be at Missing Pieces." He kissed me quickly, his handsome face flushed from the heat from the kitchen. "Can you stay for lunch?"

"I'm definitely staying until I have a chance to talk to you. Is there anything I can do?"

"Not a thing." His blue/gray eyes zeroed in on my face. "What's wrong?"

"We'll talk when you have time. It can wait."

"I'll set us up for lunch at the table over there." He nodded to what I thought of as 'our' table in a corner of the big kitchen—the best seat in the house as far as I was concerned.

"Great. I can't wait."

I really couldn't. The whole seafolk thing was about to explode out of me. I helped him get the small table set for us with plates and silverware. I snatched a few fresh rolls and smothered one with butter and honey while I was waiting.

Finally it was time for all the high school students to serve the buffet lunch. Kevin dropped salads, bread, and his Shrimp Almandine off at our table and then went to make sure everything was running smoothly inside and out before he sat down.

"That was one heck of a morning," he said with a grin. "Good idea about hiring the students for servers. That kept my cooks working in the kitchen to get the food out. I think everything is going well. Everyone seems happy. Looks like a successful open house."

"I met a merman."

He was about to say something else, his mouth opened to form the words, but they never came out. "What?"

"A merman. He said his name is Tovi. I met him last night at the house, but he was naked, and I thought he was just some drunken visitor. He grabbed me and jumped on the sandbar this morning as I walked to town hall. I saw him disappear into the water, Kevin. He had a big fish tail and really strange eyes."

"Have you eaten today?"

"If that's a nice way of asking me if I imagined the whole thing, I didn't. He was real. He said his people didn't kill Captain Lucky even though it might look that way. I didn't have a chance to tell him that no one would think that. He's coming back again tonight. I think he might only be able to be out of the water with legs from dusk to dawn—kind of like the old mermaid stories. I'm not sure about that. But he jumped in the water before the sun really came up, and he isn't coming back until tonight. I think that gives it away, don't you?"

"I don't think seafolk exist, Dae. It had to be some kind of trick."

I stared at the man I loved. "You didn't blink when I first told you about my gift. You were steadfast through a pirate ghost, a ghost ship, demon horses, me being taken over by a witch from the past, and traveling through time. But you draw the line at the idea of seafolk?"

He smiled and put his hand over mine. "When you put it that way, I suppose it sounds silly. But Anne and I worked through all kinds of supernatural phenomena, and I never heard anything mentioned about seafolk."

Kevin had a psychic partner in the FBI that had made his transition here with me easier.

"But the archives at the museum are full of stories

and drawings made from sailors' accounts. Why doesn't that make it possible?"

"I'm not saying it's not possible," he explained. "I'm saying no one has ever made contact with another species on the planet, with the exception of Mary Catherine and her kind speaking to animals."

"I didn't imagine Tovi or dream him," I defended. "He was with me in the Duck Shoppes parking lot when I ran into Peggy Lee and her husband last night. They saw him too. He was real."

"But it was at night, so he had legs."

"Are you making fun of me?" I demanded hotly. "I couldn't wait to get over here and tell you about this. I knew you'd understand, but you don't, do you?"

He shrugged his broad shoulders. "I don't know what to say. If you say you met a naked merman and talked to him, I believe you. But you're the only person in the world to ever do so."

"That doesn't make it impossible."

"True. I suppose he knew English too. Or did he have some kind of translator?"

That was it. Despite my eagerness to see him and eat the delicious lunch on the table, I grabbed another roll and left him.

"Wait, Dae." He got to his feet. "Don't leave. I'm sorry. It's been a rough morning."

"That doesn't explain you making jokes at my expense. I'm going to make some money. I'll talk to you later."

"Kevin!" One of the student servers called out his name. "Someone upset the soup tureen in the dining room, and there's soup everywhere."

"Wait," he said to me. "Don't leave until I get back.

Let's talk about this."

But I was already determined to go. As soon as he'd followed the young man toward the dining room, I stalked out the front door. I was angry and embarrassed by what he'd said to me. Kevin never acted that way. What was it about seafolk that was so hard to believe?

A woman wearing an ankle-length green cotton skirt, her long gray hair wind-tossed around her interesting face, almost ran right into me. Or I almost ran right into her. I wasn't exactly looking where I was going.

"I'm so sorry." I smiled my perfect mayor's smile and stuck my hand out in her direction. "I'm Mayor Dae O'Donnell. You don't look familiar to me. Welcome to Duck."

"Thank you so much, Mayor O'Donnell." She shook my hand in a distracted manner. "I'm Tess Horner. Dr. Tess Horner. I'm looking for the gambling ship where the man was found dead. Do you know where that is?"

"Of course. You're very close. Would you like some lunch before you go? It's free here today."

"No. Not right now, thanks. I'm very excited to be in Duck after receiving a call from a colleague who's here on vacation. Perhaps you know something about what happened on the ship?"

I studied her carefully. She didn't look like a reporter, and she'd added "Dr." to her name when she introduced herself. But why would she be interested in Captain Lucky's death?

"That's not far from here. I'm afraid the ship isn't open right now due to the investigation. Maybe you'd like to try your hand at some deep sea fishing or surfing until the police are finished."

"I should have explained who I am." Dr. Tess Horner smiled and pushed her hair back from her face. "I'm a marine biologist from the University of Minnesota. I've come all this way because my colleague feels sure your captain was killed by an aquatic human."

My eyes felt as though they were bulging out as I stared at her. "You mean a merman?" My voice could barely squeak out the words.

"I suppose you could say that." She smiled. "It is my fervent hope that we can find proof that the seafolk had a part in your captain's murder."

Chapter Ten

I glanced back toward the kitchen. Kevin was probably still in the dining room. I wanted to introduce her to him and smile broadly as she explained her mission.

Instead I told her that I knew a lot about what she was looking for and invited her to Missing Pieces for tea. Tess was happy to accompany me since I had firsthand experience with an aquatic human. We stopped and picked up sandwich bagels at the coffee shop on the way.

"So you have actually encountered a male of the species," Tess said when she was seated on my burgundy brocade sofa. "How marvelous! What did he look like? I have a thousand questions for you."

I explained the entire thread of events as best I could over lunch. Shoppers came and went, probably not getting the kind of attention I would normally have given them because I was so caught up in the idea that I had really met a merman.

"And he spoke English?" She typed notes into her tablet as we talked.

"He said he was familiar with humans and the way we lived." I shrugged. "I don't think that was accurate. Most people wouldn't even believe he existed." I sighed, thinking about my heated debate with Kevin.

"I'm afraid that's very true, Dae." Tess shook her head. "I've traveled around the world following accounts of humans or humanoid creatures that live in the sea and in fresh water. I have never been able to prove their existence."

"I've read plenty of stories about them. We should go to the Duck Historical Museum later. There have been hundreds of mermaid sightings off the coast of the Outer Banks. Always men reporting beautiful mermaids, of course." I smiled at her. "Maybe that's what makes them so hard to believe."

"Perhaps. But you have to remember that men have spent more time in related activities that brought them to the sea than women. Everything is subjective. I'd love to go to the museum and take a look at what's there. Many things that we used to think were nothing but mythology and folklore are actually true."

"Yes. And Captain Lucky did give me the coral horn that he said was used to call the seafolk. Maybe he was involved with one of them."

"A coral horn?" Her eyes got wide. "May I see it? This is all so exciting. You know, I've been to the Outer

Banks before on another sighting. But that was Hatteras Island, and I went home empty-handed."

I got the coral horn as a stream of customers came into the shop. I had to deal with them first, answering questions about different items made with seashells that I carried. Some of them were made locally, but many were not. One man and woman bought almost every local piece I had. I thanked them heartily and then went back with the horn to Tess.

"Oh, this is wonderful. Have you tried blowing into it?" She put the coral to her lips.

I put my hand on the horn. "I haven't tried it, but someone else did. It makes a terrible sound, and now I wonder if that isn't what brought the merman here."

She put it down. "It sounds as though Tovi has been here for a while, definitely before Captain Lucky died, right?"

The door chimed, and I looked up. It was Kevin. I was still a little angry with him. Before we could exchange any uneasy pleasantries, I introduced him to Tess.

"Very nice to meet you." She shook his hand. "Dae has been so helpful. You're a lucky man to be with someone with her gifts."

He smiled. "Thank you, although she'd be the first to tell you it isn't always easy."

"But then it never is, is it?" Tess smiled and looked back and forth between us. "Have you seen the merman too?"

I sat on the burgundy brocade sofa beside her and let Kevin take the chair.

"No," he answered. "It's interesting that you showed up just as he did."

"Kevin used to be with the FBI before he settled here," I explained to Tess. "He's suspicious of everyone."

"Oh!" She laughed. "You think I may have made up my search for the sea people to cover my involvement in Captain Lucky's murder?"

"I've heard crazier things," he responded, not backing down.

"So have I," she agreed. "But in this case, I can show you the text I got from the man who runs the local newspaper. I believe you'll find it's time-stamped *after* the captain's death."

"I'm not active with the FBI, and certainly not with the Duck Police." Kevin waved away the cell phone she offered him. "I spent so many years looking for puzzle pieces that I do it naturally. I apologize if I offended you."

"You didn't offend me." Tess glanced at me as she put away her cell phone and got to her feet. "Dae, I am so grateful that I ran into you. If you could arrange for me to get onboard the ship and take a look at the crime scene you described, that would be wonderful. I'd love to get a sample of that seaweed! As for this evening when Tovi said he'd return, I'd like to be here for that too. I'm staying with a friend in Duck. I'm going to let her know I'm here and drop off my stuff, but I'll be back."

"Great." I stood with her. "I'll see you later, then."

"Nice meeting you, Kevin." She shook his hand again. "Good luck."

After she was gone, Kevin and I sat quietly together. I was very excited about meeting Tess and filled to the brim with mermaid lore. I didn't want to get into that conversation with him again, but I wasn't sure I could say anything without mentioning it.

"So his name is Tovi," Kevin finally said.

"Yes."

"And he's a merman. A *naked* merman."

"Yes. At least he was naked the two times I saw him."

"Then I guess I'd like to be here when he comes back too."

"I don't want to scare him off."

"He doesn't sound very shy, Dae. He stalked you, picked you up, and jumped on the sandbar. And I assume Tess will be here. I'll be very quiet."

"It might be easier if I take a picture of him," I offered. "I'm not an FBI profiler, but it's easy to get a disbelieving vibe from you."

"Do you have to be a believer like you and Tess to see him?"

I got to my feet again. "Kevin—"

He stood too and put his arms around me. "I'm sorry. I know I'm naturally skeptical. It has nothing to do with my former career. But if you say you saw a merman—or a unicorn—I don't care. I believe you. If you don't want me to be here, I understand. But be careful in case this is some elaborate hoax you're involved in that has something to do with the murder."

I hugged him back. "I love you, skepticism and all. That's all I ask is that you believe I'm telling the truth. You don't have to believe there are seafolk—until I prove it to you."

We sat on the sofa and kissed for a while. It made us both feel better. I knew we were on the same page now. I didn't have to prove anything to him. He had my back, and that was what counted.

The door chimed, and I lazily looked over Kevin's shoulder. It was Trudy. She was wearing her wedding gown and sobbing.

"Dae, I have to talk to you. I can't marry Tim. I don't know what to do. Everything is such a mess." She scrubbed her hands over her red eyes. "Hello, Kevin. Sorry. If I'm interrupting, I can come back."

"No." He walked to her and took her arm, seating her beside me, her huge white dress poofing out around her. "I was just leaving. I'll see you later, Dae. Good luck, Trudy."

I smiled as he mimed calling him after Trudy had finished talking to me.

"I feel so awful," Trudy cried. "You have to do something, Dae. My wedding is ruined."

"Okay. Slow down. Take a deep breath. Let me make you some chamomile tea, and we'll talk."

The tea was made, but another large group of customers came into the shop. I gave Trudy the cup and told her to wait for me as I went to speak with them.

Unfortunately for me, Trudy, and the customers, they were looking for my good stuff, the icing on the cake that I sold rarely but enjoyed the most. They scrutinized every real piece I had and were enthusiastic and knowledgeable. They closely examined the rosewood tea service and Lady Spencer's teardrop earrings.

I kept looking over at Trudy to see how she was doing. It was hard to keep my mind on the pieces I was showing when she was sitting there crying. I was afraid she would leave before we had a chance to talk.

Finally my customers said they would be back after perusing other Duck antique shops. I really hated it when people said that because I knew they probably wouldn't return.

On the other hand, my lifelong best friend who was completely miserable.

There wasn't much choice. I said goodbye to my potential customers who might or might not buy something big later that would keep me in business for six months. I made sure they all had my business cards. And then I watched them leave and sat with my friend.

"I'm so sorry." I held her hand.

"You have to make money too." She sniffled and started crying again.

"What's wrong? Just pre-wedding jitters?"

"I wish that was all that was wrong." She wiped her eyes. "It was an accident. Darcy is making handkerchiefs for all the men in the wedding party. She's also renting the tuxedos. Except for Tim who's buying a tuxedo from her because he wanted to have one."

"And what happened?"

"I was there for a fitting, wearing my wedding gown." She looked down at the frothy white dress she was wearing. "Tim came in. He didn't know I was there. I saw him in the mirror behind me. I tried to get away before he saw me. We all know it's bad luck for the groom to see the bride in her dress before the wedding."

"And he saw you." I smiled and hugged her. "That doesn't mean you have to call off the wedding, Trudy. It's probably happened to dozens of brides, but their weddings went okay anyway. It's going to be fine."

She started wailing in earnest, and there was no comforting her.

"You don't understand, Dae." She finally took a breath and started speaking again. "It wasn't only that he saw me. It was what he *said* when he saw me."

"Please, Trudy, just tell me. I'm sure we can make it right."

She lifted her tearstained face to me, one of the very few times I'd ever seen Trudy's pretty face less than perfect. "He said, 'Good thing you're trying on different gowns, honey. That one you're wearing really sucks.' "

The words brought a flood of tears. She completely lost it. It took me a few minutes to calm her down again.

"He hates my wedding gown. The gown my parents spent thousands of dollars on and that Darcy has already worked on for months. He hates it, Dae. That has to mean it's over. We don't even have enough in common to like the same wedding dress."

I didn't take the opportunity to tell her that I wasn't crazy about the hoop-skirted ballroom design she'd chosen for her gown either. We'd talked about it a little when she'd first commissioned Darcy to make it. But when I saw Trudy was completely sold on the gown, I didn't say anything else about it. If there is one thing a woman should be able to choose in her life, it should be the dress she's married in.

It wouldn't help at that moment to tear her dreams down any further. So I sat and held her hand, took out a new box of tissues, and tried to get her to calm her down.

My methods seem to be working when Tim came

running through the front door so fast that the chime didn't sound until the door was closing behind him.

"Oh my God, Trudy." He knelt on the floor beside her. "I had no idea, sweetie. Darcy told me this is the gown you want. I love it. Really. It's the most beautiful gown I've ever seen."

He tried to take her hand.

She stared at him, mascara running down her face. "Love it? You said you hated it. Now you're lying to me. I knew this wedding wasn't a good idea. It's off, Tim. That's it. You and I aren't getting married."

Trudy was out the door, as fast as she could in that huge skirt. I watched her run down the boardwalk, almost knocking a few tourists off the side of the walkway and into the water.

Tim got up and sat on the sofa with his hands on his blond flat top.

"What should I do, Dae? Nobody knows her better than you. What can I say to make this right?"

"I don't know. Maybe you should just leave her alone for a while and let her get over it. A wedding dress, or anything to do with a wedding, is very emotional. I think I might skip the whole thing when it's time for me and Kevin."

Tim got on his feet, six-foot-six, thin and wiry. His blue eyes stared down into mine.

"I have to do something. What if she doesn't get over it? She needs someone to talk to."

"But not you," I discouraged. "Let her talk to her mother and her aunt. They're close. Maybe they can change her mind."

"You know I respect you, Dae. I always have, even though you do some crazy things sometimes. We've known each other all our lives. Heck, I thought it would be me and you getting married. But I just feel in my gut that I should find her and beg her to forgive me. Thanks for your help anyway."

There was no stopping him. He left the shop in the same haste he'd entered. I wished them both a lot of luck, and then I looked at the almanac to see what time sunset was that night.

Chapter Eleven

The rest of the day was super busy. I was afraid the Fourth of July crowds might buy everything I had. It was exciting but also made me anxious. What would I open with tomorrow? Sometimes it took me months to bring in new merchandise. If I had poor stock, I might have to be closed the next day.

Toward the end of the afternoon, Mary Catherine came into the shop with Peggy Lee and her husband. I was happy to see them and have a chance to explain about what had happened before and after the town hall meeting.

Peggy and Mary Catherine were tea drinkers like me. Steve, Peggy's husband, had a cold Pepsi from my mini-fridge.

"Did you find the naked man from the parking lot?" Steve asked.

"I saw him again later," I explained but didn't go any further. After Kevin's reaction, I thought Steve and Peggy might feel the same. "People are looking into it. Thanks for asking."

"Mary Catherine thought we might all go out to dinner tonight," Peggy suggested. "We're hoping to meet your ex-FBI fiancé."

"That sounds great." I mentally calculated what time that could be. Sundown would be at about eight-thirty, according to the almanac. If we had dinner early, both things could still happen. "Would six or six-thirty be all right? Kevin runs the Blue Whale Inn, and he has open house all day so he won't have to cook dinner tonight. I'm sure he'd love to go."

We talked about it a little more and made plans to meet at Wild Stallions. Peggy and Steve left, but Mary Catherine remained.

"I've heard a few strange things from some of my friends," she told me. "One of the turtles that live around the sandbar said he saw you with a merman before sunrise this morning."

I'm sure my eyes got big. "You know about the seafolk?"

"Well I don't know any *personally*. I've heard from many different sources that they're very private people, very shy of humans. Not that I blame them. No doubt we'd do terrible things to them if science ever found one."

Thinking about Tess, I wondered if I'd made a mistake. "Maybe not every scientist," I hedged. "But that's wonderful that you believe me. Kevin made a big fuss about me telling him that I'd seen a merman. My feelings were hurt that he wasn't willing to take my word for it."

"It's probably just as well." Her brows knit together above her green eyes. "What did the merman want with you? Did you just happen to see him, or was there a reason he looked for you?"

I told her everything, including what Tovi had said about war between humans and seafolk. "I think he's too innocent about us to realize how devastating it would be for his people to come out of hiding and think they could fight us."

"It would be bad for everyone," she agreed. "I wonder why he bothered telling you about Captain Lucky? Do you think he killed him? You said yourself that the room was covered in seaweed and such. Maybe he drowned him and put that other stuff around to claim the deed. Who knows how mermen are?"

I changed the subject as I questioned her about Peggy Lee.

"How do you know her?"

Mary Catherine laughed. "I helped her with her Great Dane many years ago. But I never forget a dog face. I knew him right away. I was really glad to see him again and hear that he's doing so well. Peggy and her husband brought Shakespeare to my shop this afternoon. It's always a pleasure to see a former client and know that I helped in some small way."

"That's an amazing story." The chime sounded at the front door, and a young couple came in looking for some bargain souvenirs.

Mary Catherine went back to the Pet Emporium,

and I waited on my last customers for the day. I had an idea about going home and rummaging in the attic to see if I could find anything interesting, and yet not sentimental, to sell in Missing Pieces during the big weekend. I decided to close early, go home, and look around before I changed clothes and met everyone for dinner.

On the way home from the Duck Shoppes, I called Kevin, and he was fine with dinner at Wild Stallions. He was interested in meeting Steve too, as I thought he would be. I knew Gramps might want to go too, since Mary Catherine was going to be there. He might not have been in the FBI, but he liked talking about that stuff as much as Kevin did.

I was pleased to see that he was home when I got there. I ran in the front door and found him having a quick snack from the microwave.

"I'm glad to see you, Chief O'Donnell." I smiled and hugged him. "How was your day at work?"

"It was good, except for the murder investigation. I tried to take a few clues from what you'd said about Captain Lucky needing money to get out of town." He sighed as he sat down with his warmed up fish stew. "Tuck and I paid a few visits to all the local people who loan money or keep some big poker games going. We figured maybe Captain Lucky owed some money to one of them. None of them knew him. Are you sure that's what he told you?"

I sat at the table with him. "That's what he said. I'm sorry you didn't get a lead from that, but maybe it's someone on the mainland. Wouldn't it be odd that Captain Lucky ran a gambling ship and didn't do his gambling right there?"

Gramps shrugged. "Maybe he didn't want to do it at home, so to speak."

I stopped him before he took his first bite of stew. "We're going out to dinner around six with some friends of Mary Catherine's. I thought you might want to go."

"It would look bad for the chief of police to be out eating dinner when he hasn't figured out who killed a popular figure in the community. I'm just grabbing this to keep going. But thanks, honey. Have a good time."

"People don't expect the chief of police not to have a life because he's working on a case. You can't go 24/7 on it."

He grunted. "I know this business, Dae. I'm doing what I need to do."

I told him about Tim and Trudy. He didn't seem surprised.

"Tim told me all about it. I'm glad your grandmother and I ran away to get married."

"You ran away? I didn't know that. Were your relatives against your marriage or something?"

"No. We both came from large families right here in Duck. Neither one of us wanted the big deal marriage everyone wanted us to have. No one had the money for it either. It was easier just getting in the car and going to Wilmington." He smiled. "I think we enjoyed it more too."

I covered his hand with mine. As long as I could remember, that soft look had come into his eyes when he mentioned Grandma Eleanore. I knew he still loved her.

"Missing Pieces almost sold out today." I changed the subject. "I thought I might go through the attic and see what I can find."

"Good idea since most of that junk up there is yours anyway. They could've had you on one of those hoarding reality shows when you were a teenager. You know what's good. Get rid of the rest if you can. There were big crowds at the parade today. I'm glad for the town, but we were really stretched thin with the murder investigation too."

"There's a marine biologist on vacation here. I was telling her about the weird ocean stuff on the ship around Captain Lucky. What would you think if she took a look at it to see if she can identify any of it?"

"I don't see what it could hurt, but I'd want to see her credentials first to make sure she's not a journalist or something. The company that owns the Andalusia is really worried about this affecting their operations here. It's not helping that they have to be closed down for the investigation either. I hope those crime scene people from Manteo finish up there tonight."

"Great. I'll tell her. Thanks, Gramps."

I asked him how Chief Michaels was doing and his terse reply was, "As good as can be expected."

"I'll try my best to get over there tomorrow. Chris sent flowers from the town."

Grabbing a cookie from the jar on the cabinet, I started upstairs.

"When were you planning on telling me about the naked man in the parking lot?"

"There wasn't much to tell," I lied. I definitely didn't want to talk about seafolk with him.

"I didn't see any calls to the police department about it, Dae. I wouldn't even know except that MC told me. I think you should've reported this."

"Gramps, you know how crazy some people get on vacation. He didn't try to hurt me."

"But she said he showed up here and followed you to the parking lot." He frowned. "I haven't had any other calls, but I want you to file a report first thing tomorrow morning."

"Couldn't this be my report?"

"No." His mouth was tight. "I can't believe you'd even ask me that. Go to the police department. It's in the same building as your office. It's not that hard."

"This is what I remember about my grandfather being sheriff of Dare County," I said. "I never got away with anything."

He chuckled, breaking the tension. "And you never will. See you tonight or tomorrow, honey. Take care."

Treasure was sleeping on one of the stairs. He followed me to the attic and walked carefully across the dusty floor, lifting his paws and shaking them every time he encountered a dust bunny.

We rarely used the attic. It was storage for all the old things we didn't want but couldn't bear to throw away. I was pretty sure there were still things up here from Gramps's childhood and definitely from my own.

I switched on the overhead light. It barely made shadows in the large room. It was hard to search for anything in particular up here since I wanted to look at everything.

My great-grandmother's wedding dress was still stored in a pretty trunk. It even had her flowered headdress and a yellowed lace veil. I picked up her tiny satin shoes and marveled at the size of her feet. Mine were so much bigger!

Touching her things without gloves was a pleasant

experience. I saw her and my great-grandfather getting married in the old chapel by the sea that had once stood on the beach. I wasn't present there, like I was with Grandma Eleanore, but it was fun.

There were two good mantel clocks that I remembered finding when I was in my early twenties, before I'd opened Missing Pieces. I didn't know who they had originally belonged to—I couldn't touch things back then and learn their past.

They were harmless enough once I touched them. One had belonged to a retired shop owner in Charleston and the other to a widow in Newport News.

Gramps was right about the large amount of missing things that I'd found and stashed up there. Some of the items came from walks on the beach—a carved ship in an old bottle and a diamond engagement ring.

I held the ring to see who it belonged to. It was a beautiful, expensive ring that I was sure someone hated to lose. I immediately felt cold and shaky, my usual response to holding anything I could get information from.

It was surprising when I saw that the ring belonged to Mrs. Euly Stanley. It had been her engagement ring.

I smiled at the image of a much younger Euly Stanley as she allowed her suitor to put the ring on her finger. I blinked my eyes once I knew where the ring belonged and put it in my pocket to be returned the next time I saw her.

Curiously, there was very little emotion behind the ring. It had nothing to do with age. Many of the things I found had very passionate emotions lodged in them even though they were hundreds of years old. Mrs.

Stanley was a little cool toward her husband when he gave her the ring. She didn't dislike him, but she didn't love him either.

There were many boxes of unusual rocks and seashells that I'd found. I took one of those boxes with me too. Seashells were getting harder to find along the beach. This was a good collection of them to sell to tourists.

There was the old organ that hadn't worked as long as I could remember. And an ironing board that was covered with someone's old dress. Gramps had told me the story about how that came to be here, but while an amusing family anecdote, it was hardly salable material.

I found a small wood trunk and opened it carefully. There were a few old pictures in it, a crumbling flower, and a pink garter.

From the pictures, I knew this was Gramps and Grandma Eleanore's runaway wedding. There were several postcards from Wilmington and one very clear shot of the young couple. They were posing, from the looks of it, immediately after they were married.

I sat back on my heels, feeling the strength of their love and the pull of this moment in the past. There was also a strange aura of warning that made me drop the picture of them. I couldn't define what it was—like a cloud in my mind. But I knew I would have to come back to it later.

Putting everything back in the trunk, I put it in my growing pile to take downstairs.

By the time I was finished in the attic, I'd found some interesting family heirlooms, possibly the most important of them—my mother's youthful treasure box with the rainbow unicorn inside. There was also a plastic bracelet, and her tickets to the carnival Grandma Eleanore had referred to.

One of the tickets was an entrance to see the Amazing Anthony, the psychic that I might use as a guide to help me speak with my mother and warn her against going home the night after our fight when I was in college.

It took me about thirty minutes to take everything downstairs from the attic, with a follow up shower to get all the dust and cobwebs off me. I figured I'd have to borrow the golf cart to transport all of it to the shop the next day. By that time, I'd have everything shined up and polished. Maybe it wouldn't be a bad day at Missing Pieces tomorrow after all.

I changed clothes, wearing a long, cotton wraparound skirt in a vivid shade of blue. My white top was casual but dressy and showed off my tan as it draped off one shoulder. I put on a little lipstick and ran a comb through my hair. That was as good as it was going to get.

Treasure meowed from the bed as I put on a new pair of white sandals.

"I'm so sorry, but things have been hectic. I'll take you to Missing Pieces tomorrow for sure. And Baylor won't be there. Okay?"

He didn't sound moved by my promises. Instead he jumped down from the bed and wandered into the hall. He looked carefully both ways, still not liking Mary Catherine's cat springing out at him with no warning. I'd thought he might just have to get used to Baylor being around, but when I married Kevin and moved to the Blue Whale, he wouldn't have that problem.

I carefully looked around myself as I went down the familiar stairs to the kitchen and living room. The house was old and worn, but it was everything I'd ever known. It wasn't going to be easy going to live with Kevin, but I hoped the perks that came with it would be worth it.

As I walked to Wild Stallions, I chided myself about getting old and set in my ways. I was reluctant to give up my childhood home for a wonderful man, possibly a family of my own, and the great old inn that was a remarkable spot.

"I don't know what more you could ask for," I said to myself. "As changes go, this one could be awesome."

Peggy and Steve were fun to chat with over dinner. Her work trying to create plants that would help feed the world—and her reluctant stories about working as a forensic botanist to solve murders—were fascinating. Mary Catherine, as usual, added her own brand of charm to the conversation and talked about recent families she'd enlightened about their pets.

I told stories of pirates and treasures and even did a small example of my ability by guessing that Peggy's watch had been a gift from her father.

Kevin and Steve barely noticed that we were there at all. Their conversation was intense and quiet but only between them. Peggy muttered that we should have made them sit farther apart at the table. Both men looked up when we laughed at that.

All the while, I kept my eyes on the setting sun and the smooth gray water of the Currituck Sound, watching for a head to bob up or a large tail that cleaved the water.

Chapter Twelve

After dinner, Peggy and Steve went back to their friends' house where they were staying. Mary Catherine hung around, trying to decide if she should stay to see the merman.

"Perhaps four of us might be a bit much for Tovi." She stared over the edge of the boardwalk where the kayaks launched. Hundreds of fish were jumping out of the water trying to get her attention.

"I don't know. He says he knows humans. He must know we think there's safety in numbers." I smiled at her.

"She might have a point," Kevin said. "Whatever he has planned might not happen if there are too many of us around to stop him."

"I don't think I can convince Tess not to be there," I said. "She's waited all her life for this."

"I'm just going home," Mary Catherine decided. "I suppose Horace will be gone until late."

"Probably so." I told her about our encounter at the house. "He takes being chief as seriously as he did being sheriff. He won't rest until he knows what happened to Captain Lucky."

Kevin nodded. "That's his job. I'm sure you wouldn't want him to be any different with it."

Mary Catherine and I smiled at each other.

"All right then. I'm going home to read a little and give Baylor some extra attention," she said. "I'll see you later, Dae. Be careful. I've heard that the seafolk can be impatient with humans and even ferocious."

"I will." I saw Tess coming toward us on the boardwalk. "I'll tell you about it later."

Kevin was going to stay. "I'll sit in the corner, and he won't even know I'm here. I don't want to leave you alone with him, Dae."

"She won't be alone," Tess said. "I know about what we're dealing with. I won't let either of us get into any trouble."

"Thanks but I'll feel better if I stay. I suppose this is something you've always hoped for, seeing a real merman."

"Oh yes. A lifetime fascination for me."

"I promise not to disturb your study of the undersea life."

"That's fine, Kevin," I finally told him. "I don't think two extra people will bother Tovi. He seemed very outgoing. Let's go inside. I told him I'd wait for him there."

We went into Missing Pieces, and Kevin was as good as his word, sitting in a chair toward the back of the shop while Tess and I sat on the burgundy brocade sofa. I left the front door open for my guest, my heart starting to beat faster as I realized he could be there at any time.

"Maybe I should put on some water for tea," I said nervously.

"I doubt Tovi will want our tea," Tess said. "I'm sure his diet is much different than ours."

"Do you have any idea what antargatis means?" I asked her. "A friend of mine heard it mentioned, and we were wondering if it has anything to do with seafolk."

"It's a very old term for what may have been the first seafolk," she said. "I've never heard them referred to by that name—only in text books. Where did your friend hear it?"

A gust of wind blew in from the sound. Pairs of people laughed as they walked, arm-in-arm along the boardwalk in the twinkling lights that came on right after sunset. Scents of cooking food mingled with the smell of the water.

And then there was a figure in the doorway—not Tovi.

"I am Lilly, Tovi's sister. Are you Dae O'Donnell?"

I stood up and approached her.

Lilly was similar to her brother in height but had a smaller build. She was pale too, and her eyes changed color. But she had long greenish-tinged white hair that ended around her waist. She was as naked as Tovi had been.

"I'm Mayor Dae O'Donnell," I introduced myself.

"It's very nice to meet you."

"And I'm Dr. Tess Horner." Tess put out one hand to the mermaid.

Lilly looked away, possibly not recognizing the custom.

"I apologize that my brother couldn't be here. He was kept away and asked me to come in his stead. What is it that you wish of us?"

Tess giggled, but immediately put a hand over her mouth.

"Tovi was talking to me about the death of a friend of mine—Captain Lucky," I said. "We were going to meet to talk further about it."

She held her pointed chin high and stared at me coldly with her ever-changing eyes. "Your captain was even less than human and deserved to die."

I saw Kevin slowly get to his feet and stand beside his chair.

"Surely you don't mean that," I suggested to her. "You didn't even know Captain Lucky. Tovi was worried that we might think one of your people killed him. Do you know anything about that?"

Lilly was looking at Kevin but didn't back down. "No doubt my brother killed him so that I would not need to."

"Why would your brother want to kill him?" Tess asked.

"Because he made a fool of me." Lilly turned sharply toward her. "Humans and my kind were never meant to meet. Do not summon one of us again with the coral horn. Only disaster and death can come of it."

The three of us watched as Lilly turned and ran off the end of the boardwalk. Her splash attracted curious eyes as Tess, Kevin, and I looked off the side rail.

"Look there!" Tess shouted. "I see her."

Kevin's eyes followed where she pointed. We both saw the large blue and gold tail come out of the water as Lilly dove down and disappeared.

Tess put her hand to her forehead. "Oh my God! I can't believe it. I finally saw a mermaid."

"At least you saw a woman you believed to be a mermaid based on what Dae told you about a merman," Kevin said.

She rounded on him. "I took pictures. Did she look human to you?"

He shrugged. "There are lots of different-looking humans, Dr. Horner, as I'm sure you're aware."

"I know what I saw. I knew what I was looking for," she argued. "We'll get more proof. You'll see. Even skeptics like you will be convinced."

There were a few of the same blue, orange, and gold scales that I'd picked up from the pier the day Captain Lucky had died. I pointed them out to Tess who immediately put on gloves and opened plastic cases she'd had in her bag to take samples.

"What happened to the seafolk being friendly?" Kevin asked as we went back into Missing Pieces.

"Tovi was friendly, in a way. Obviously his sister, not so much."

"I know you and Dr. Horner feel like this is a miracle, but I still think it's a scam. It's possible Lilly actually killed Captain Lucky and is setting us up to think a mermaid did it. You said the death looked like it was staged, Dae. She might have killed him and then come up with this idea to get out of it."

"I don't think that's what this is, Kevin. I don't

understand Tovi and Lilly's involvement with this, but I believe they do live in the sea."

"Keeping the whole seafolk thing out of it, Captain Lucky was known for his romantic affairs. I know they've ruled out the gambling angle, but being dumped by the most popular man in town is definitely one of the oldest reasons for murder."

"I haven't told Gramps about this." I glanced toward the door where Tess was still collecting samples. "I didn't think he'd appreciate the mermaid angle either."

"But he might appreciate anyone going to so much trouble to make herself appear innocent," he concluded. "I think you should tell Horace about it."

"I'll think about it."

Tess came back in raptures about the samples she'd found.

"This could be more conclusive than seeing one of them." She held one of the small plastic boxes up to the light. "I can't wait to examine it."

My cell phone rang. It was Gramps.

"Dae, if you want to take your friend the biologist out to the Andalusia, you're gonna have to do it tonight. Crime scene techs are finished, and a judge has agreed to let the ship sail again tomorrow."

"Thanks. We can do that." I glanced at Tess and explained that we would have to go to the ship right away before everything was cleaned up.

"That's fine with me, Dae." Tess grabbed her bag. "This is all I came for and more than I expected. Thank you."

Kevin insisted on going with us. I knew Gramps didn't care since he often asked for Kevin's opinion on things, just like Chief Michaels and Sheriff Riley did.

We rode over to the gambling ship in Kevin's blue golf cart with signs painted all over it for the Blue Whale. There were still crowds in the streets. It was no wonder that the owners of the Andalusia wanted to reopen and take advantage of the thousands of people here for the weekend.

Tim was stationed at the end of the long pier that led to the ship. He still looked angry and confused. I knew him well enough to know that nothing had changed between him and Trudy.

"She's still saying it's off," he told me as Tess and I waited for Kevin to park the golf cart. "She says I don't know her well enough which means she doesn't know me well enough. How am I supposed to get past that, Dae? It's bad enough that her parents hate me."

"Trudy's parents don't hate you," I advised. "They just want what's best for her."

"And that's not me. I get it. I wasn't even good enough to take over for Chief Michaels. Instead they hired someone from outside the department who's probably too old to work."

I lifted a brow.

"Sorry. I got carried away. Of course your grandfather is in good shape and can handle this. But I know that's what Trudy's parents are thinking."

"Mating rituals are always complicated," Tess said. "But usually the male that doesn't give up is the winner of the female's affections."

"Thanks." Tim didn't look as though he had any idea what she was talking about.

Kevin joined us, and it was another ride on a cart, a shiny gold one, up to the boarding ramp. All the lights on the Andalusia were on, making a gorgeous display in the darkness.

Gramps was waiting on the ship for us. I introduced him to Tess, and he shook hands with Kevin.

"I hope you'll be able to tell us something about what happened here, Dr. Horner," Gramps said as we walked together to the stateroom.

"I'll do my best, Chief O'Donnell, though you may not care for my theories."

He frowned and glanced at me. I shrugged and looked the other way. I just told him she wanted a look at it. I knew he wouldn't like it when she started talking about seafolk.

The large room appeared almost the same as the last time I'd seen it—no Captain Lucky on the bed, thank goodness. Everything else was still covered in various forms of sea life. It was dried now as it hadn't been when I'd found him.

"This is fascinating." Tess walked slowly around the room, peering at everything as though it was already under a microscope. "And you say the whole room was soaking wet when you found him?"

"Yes. The rugs squished under my feet, and the walls and ceiling were wet to the touch. It reminded me of that time we pulled what was left of that old boat out of the water at the beach. Remember, Gramps?"

He nodded. "It was still like that when I came on the case. It's dried a lot now, but some of it was wiped down by the crime scene techs too. I don't have anything back on that information yet. But the ME says cause of death was definitely drowning. He had a sharp blow to his head which probably rendered him groggy or unconscious, but wasn't cause of death. We think he fell into the water after that. Captain Lucky had seawater in his lungs. It probably happened off this pier."

I thought about the scales I'd found on the pier. I knew then that they belonged to the seafolk.

Kevin frowned at me. I knew what he was thinking—Lilly drowned Captain Lucky and then pretended to be a mermaid. In that theory, I supposed Tovi would be her accomplice.

"I can well imagine." Tess kept looking around. "Would it be all right if I take some of my own samples, Chief O'Donnell?"

"I don't see why not, since a cleanup crew is standing by until I give the order, and then the room will be turned out and scrubbed. We have everything we need."

"Thank you so much." Tess took out more sample boxes and filled them with bits of everything she found.

"Any theories, Dr. Horner?" Gramps asked.

"Well, you see this very dark plant over here. You may not be aware of it, but it grows only at the deepest parts of the sea. It's not something you'd pull up while fishing, unless you were deep sea fishing. Someone purposely put this here. I'm sure Captain Lucky didn't go that far down off the pier."

"Killers have done stranger things to lead the police astray," Kevin remarked.

Gramps agreed with him.

"There are other oddities too," Tess continued. "I believe someone was trying to frighten your captain. This was probably done before his death. I don't believe these specimens would have dried so quickly in the humid environment Dae has described unless it had happened a day or two before."

"Maybe that was why Captain Lucky was so rattled and wanted to get out of town," I suggested.

"That doesn't make any sense, Dae," Gramps replied. "Who would threaten someone with a bunch of seaweed?"

"I don't know," I said, though I could guess. "What if it was something else?"

"I can't imagine one of the seafolk needing human money," Tess said. "I assume that's what you're proposing, Dae."

Gramps did an almost humorous double-take. "What? Seafolk? Is that what we're talking about?"

"Of course." Tess was very clear about it. "Dae met with a male of the species that seemed to be speaking about the captain's death and then tonight the female was certainly clear about threatening Captain Lucky."

"Is this true?" Gramps stared at me. "Are you talking about *mermaids*? You think mermaids killed Captain Lucky?"

"Not a mermaid *per se*," Tess said. "They were male and female, easy to see since they were both naked."

Gramps cleared his throat. "Excuse us, folks. Dae and I need to have a word alone on deck."

Chapter Thirteen

I ducked out of the stateroom with Gramps—though it felt more like I was with Chief O'Donnell—a curious distinction.

"Exactly what kind of marine biologist is Dr. Horner?" he demanded.

"The usual kind, I imagine. Her hobby is looking for proof that there are people who live in the sea."

"You could've told me that." He let out a long sigh. "You know, people are expecting me to be too old to handle this position. You didn't have to help them make me look stupid. What were you thinking?"

"I was thinking that she could help you with solving Captain Lucky's death."

"By blaming it on mermaids?" He stalked up and

down the deck a few times. "I get that you're not comfortable with me taking Ronnie's place as chief. I wouldn't have thought you'd come up with something so creative to point it out for me."

"I wasn't pointing anything out. There are seafolk, Gramps. That's who the naked man was. I saw him jump into the sound and not come back up until a big blue and gold tail sent him deeper into the water. I saw basically the same thing tonight."

"Go home, Dae. We'll figure this out without the theatrics. I'll see you later."

"Come on. You're as bad as Kevin. You can stretch your mind to imagining so many things—why not mermaids?"

I remembered the angry look on his face from when I was a child and had done something wrong.

"We'll talk about this later. Go on home."

Gramps went back into the stateroom and sent Tess and Kevin out. I had expected something like this from him, which was why I hadn't told him in the first place. Maybe it was just me. Maybe they were right, and I was too gullible.

But then they hadn't seen what Tovi had done. It was more impressive than what Lilly had done. Kevin wasn't there when Tovi had picked me up like I was a rag doll and jumped over the boardwalk to the sandbar. Maybe if he had, he'd be a believer too.

Tess looked confused too, but she didn't say anything as Tim took us back down to the end of the pier in the golf cart. When we were alone, she let it all out.

"I wasn't expecting anything more, Dae, even though he's your grandfather," she said as Kevin guided the Blue Whale cart back down to Duck Road.

"Can I give you a lift to your friend's house, Dr. Horner?" Kevin asked.

"Of course. Thank you. She lives on Sand Dollar Lane. I'll point out the house when we get there."

Kevin was silent after that as we buzzed through the dark night.

Tess and I spoke quietly about the things she'd seen and identified at the ship.

"I think it's very clear that Tovi may have tried to send Captain Lucky a message to stay away from his sister. When that didn't work, he killed him." Tess tapped her chin. "You did say he was strong and fast, besides being a creature of the water. How hard would it be for him to drown the captain and place him in the stateroom to be found?"

"But why would Tovi come to warn me about trouble? Why not just steer clear of it and leave the area? He doesn't have to be here."

"I don't know," she admitted. "But I assume there are certain boundaries that the seafolk have established to keep themselves safe from humans. Otherwise they would have been killed off centuries ago. Maybe a human relationship with one of their kind is one of those boundaries."

There were still too many things that didn't make sense to me. Kevin and I dropped Tess off at one of the cute little beach houses that had weathered storms for years. Tess and I agreed to meet the next day for coffee and discuss what she'd found at the ship.

"I know this is a hard time for you since you're mayor of Duck and your grandfather is the police chief, but I have to tell you, I'm so excited about this find.

Thank you for taking me into your confidence, Dae. Goodnight, Kevin."

When she was gone, Kevin didn't move the golf cart right away.

"Come back to my place for a while," he invited. "Let's have a few drinks."

His hand on mine, I wanted to agree, but I was worried that our conversation would become a discussion about me believing in seafolk and him not believing in them.

"I'd love to," I said with a smile. "But I really should go see Trudy and try to find a way to work this out. The next party is only a few days away. I don't want to see this breakup spiral into something bigger. Tim always wanted to marry me before he realized Trudy was his soulmate. I'd rather not go back to those days again."

"I knew Tim had his eye on you from the moment I met the two of you. I knew you weren't interested in him, so I didn't see him as much of a threat."

"In other words, you ignored him, thinking there was no rival for my affections," I said.

"Something like that. When you dated Luke Helms, that was different."

"We only dated one time."

"Yes. But by that time, I knew that I loved you. I hoped Luke wouldn't sweep you off your feet before I got my chance."

"Luke is nice enough. But he didn't stand a chance against you." I kissed him. "Owning the Blue Whale makes you very attractive marriage material. Luke lives in an apartment. I wouldn't leave my home for that."

Kevin laughed and backed the golf cart out of the

drive. "Okay. As long as we're clear on all that. Just remember that I still love you even if I don't agree with you about some things. Your grandfather still loves you too."

"I know. Thanks for the reminder. I love you too, even though you're wrong."

He glanced at me in surprise. "I think that's all anyone can ask for in a relationship. Do you want me to go to Trudy's with you?"

"You can drop me off. It might be a while. And I don't think we could have the girl chat we need to have with you there. Sorry."

"That's okay. But I expect Trudy to do the same for us when you get cold feet before our wedding."

"Me?" It was my turn to be surprised. "What about *you*? You might be the one who gets scared."

He put his arm around me and drew me close. "I've had a lot more experience in the world, Dae. I know what I want. Sometimes I'm just not sure if you do."

I didn't answer that. Of course he was wrong. I had always known what I wanted. That was why I'd never dated men who didn't live here, because I didn't want to leave my home. It was one reason I loved Kevin. He'd put down roots here.

He dropped me off at Trudy's house about three blocks away. I waved goodbye as he left, watching the tiny blue lights on the golf cart disappear before I went to knock on her door.

Kevin was wrong about me. I knew exactly what I wanted.

Trudy, however, was a complete mess. Her parents answered my knock on the front door with worried faces.

"We're so glad to see you, Dae," her father said. "Please come in."

"If that's Tim, I don't want to see him," Trudy called out.

"It's Dae, sweetheart," her mother yelled and then whispered to me, "go on back. I hope you can help her figure this out."

I followed the familiar path back to Trudy's bedroom where we'd first played with dolls together and later giggled about boys we liked. Her door was open, and I went in with all the confidence of a military leader marshalling her forces.

"I'm not sure I want to see you either, Dae." Trudy had two pillows stuffed against her face. "If you're here to talk me into marrying Tim, you might as well leave."

"I'm not here to talk you into anything." I sat on the bed beside her. "I'm here because you're my friend and something's wrong."

That was enough to make her sit up. She looked terrible. I hadn't seen Trudy look this bad in a long time. Her platinum blond hair was standing on end, and her face seemed permanently tearstained. It was also rare to see her with no makeup.

"Thanks for coming." She sniffed and swung her legs over the edge of the bed. "I don't know what I was thinking. Why was I going to marry Tim, of all people? It hasn't been that long since he wanted to marry you. I must have lost my mind."

I hugged her. "Thank goodness you finally found it."

She looked puzzled. "What do you mean? You didn't want me to marry Tim?"

"Of course not. That's why I didn't marry him, even though he asked me a hundred times."

"Why didn't you tell me?"

"Because you seemed happy with him." I shrugged. "I didn't want you to leave him if things were going well."

"Oh!"

"It's so good to have you back. I was hoping you'd dump him before you got to the altar. You know how everyone talks when that happens."

She smiled. "You're right. This is a good thing. There aren't a lot of gifts to give back yet. There's the dress, but there's nothing I can do about that."

"But better for your parents to lose money on that dress than for you to get stuck with a big loser."

Her blue eyes widened dramatically. "That's a little harsh, don't you think? I don't want to marry Tim, but I wouldn't call him a loser."

"What else can you call someone who has been on the police force for years with no promotion? He's a volunteer firefighter—no money there."

"But I admire him for that, don't you? Not everything that doesn't pay is unimportant."

"I suppose that might be his one admirable quality." I giggled. "Remember last year when he found that injured gull at his house and spent all summer nursing it back to health? I mean, what kind of man does that?"

"He's sensitive," she defended. "And he likes animals."

"Maybe that's it." I shook my head. "And that thing he has about acting like every woman he dates is a queen or something. That can get annoying."

"I like when he opens the car door and holds my jacket for me." She pushed her messy hair out of her face. "You're being really hard on him, Dae."

"How can you say that? He didn't even respect the tradition of not seeing the bride in her wedding dress before the ceremony. I think that says it all."

Trudy got to her feet. "Who believes in those silly superstitions anyway? I know lots of people who didn't even have a big wedding, and they're just fine. My parents eloped, and they've been married over thirty years."

"I just found out that Gramps and Grandma Eleanore eloped too. They got married in Wilmington because they both had such big families and didn't want a big wedding."

"Are you saying you think Tim and I should elope?"

"No! I'm saying you're lucky to be rid of him—big, tall, idiot that he is."

She hit me with one of her pillows. "You're doing this on purpose. This is one of your anti-everything speeches that you always used in high school. You really want me to marry Tim, don't you?"

"Only if you really love him. I want what's best for you." I smiled and hugged her.

"I do think Tim and I are good for each other," she whispered. "He's not all dark and mysterious like Kevin. I wouldn't know what to do with someone like him."

As we clung together, I whispered back, "He says I don't know what I want. He says I'm going to get cold feet before we get married."

Trudy took a step away from me but still held my

hands. "If you do, I'll come and talk to you, just like you came to talk to me. But, Dae, are you really sure Kevin *is* right for you?"

Chapter Fourteen

I thought a lot about that question as I walked through Duck on my way home. Trudy's father offered to take me, but I wanted time to think about everything. The best way I knew to think was walking by myself. I stared up at the crescent moon.

Trudy was right about Kevin being darker and deeper than Tim. That was another thing that I loved about him. Tim could never understand or hope to deal with the gifts life had given me. I needed that strength and stability behind me. I needed someone who could handle the things that happened to me — possibly excluding mermaids.

Tim and Trudy had been my friends forever, but there were many things I couldn't share with them.

Kevin was different. He was like Gramps. I could tell either of them anything, and most of the time, they were there for me.

I knew I wouldn't be the one backing out of the wedding, whenever it took place. But I worried a little about Kevin.

Living in Duck was a much different life for him. Would he get tired of being an innkeeper and want to go back to his exciting career with the FBI? Would he look around at our small town ways at some point and wonder why he ever thought he should stay here?

Only time would answer these questions. I couldn't be afraid to love him in case the answers weren't in my favor. And I wouldn't rush the wedding to try to hold on to him. I was a great believer in letting things unfold. This was one of those things.

Changing my mind, I started toward the Blue Whale, intending to see Kevin again that night. I quietly cut through Agnes Caudle's yard to shave some time off the trip.

I was surprised to see my old friend, Cathi Connor, again. She was walking quickly down the deserted street, head bent as though she was on a mission. I might not have recognized her if she wouldn't have been wearing the same jacket I'd seen her wearing at the firehouse after the parade.

She was headed past the Blue Whale, turning enough that I knew she was going to the Andalusia. The only thing I could imagine going on there was workers cleaning the captain's stateroom.

Quietly, I followed her. She stopped at the end of the long pier that led to the ship and stared into the water for several minutes. I waited behind the ticket office in the shadows so I could watch her.

A woman—it had to be Lilly—walked slowly out of the water. She approached Cathi from behind. I almost let out a warning cry. But then she looked up and ran to her. They hugged each other close for several moments before they sat on a bench and started talking.

While I could clearly see them, I had no idea what they were saying to one another. I wished I had some kind of surveillance gear that could let me in on their conversation.

They'd obviously known each other for a while. Their heads bent close together, they looked like sisters plotting something.

Was this somehow related to Captain Lucky's death?

It was possible this was their usual meeting place. Maybe Captain Lucky had seen them together and said he'd tell the world about mermaids. Maybe Lilly had used the water and the seaweed to threaten him.

But maybe she'd killed him to keep him quiet too.

Why hit him on the head to toss him into the water, though? She could have easily just pushed him in and held him down.

I watched the women until they got up and walked toward one of the houses close to the ship. It was a rental property—Cathi owned it. They disappeared inside and didn't come out again.

I started back the way I had come. I didn't notice that I wasn't alone until Lilly was walking beside me. For someone who normally didn't have legs, she was very quiet.

"Spying on me?" she accused. "Good things don't

happen to humans who spy on seafolk."

"From what I've read, humans and seafolk have mingled for generations, probably since men went out in boats for the first time. Tovi said your people have laws against being with humans, but that doesn't make us enemies, does it?"

"Most of my people agree that we shouldn't mate with humans. Tovi won't listen. He's asking for terrible retribution. His girlfriend too."

"His girlfriend? Is that Cathi? Did you kill Captain Lucky to protect yourself?"

The moon shone down on her pale hair. She turned quickly to face me, one strong arm out to bar me from moving forward.

"How dare you? I should drag you out to sea by the hair and drown you."

"Is that how you drowned Captain Lucky?" I pressed, despite the threat. "Who is his girlfriend?"

She shook me by the shoulders, as Tovi had.

"You don't know anything. You'd better hope it stays that way if you want to remain alive."

My last look at her was her half-shadowed face before she ran back toward the water. I heard a large splash, probably as she returned to her home.

I didn't waste any time waiting to see if she'd return. I ran the rest of the way to the Blue Whale and used the secret key Kevin kept hidden for his late arrivals and party-goers who stayed out longer than he wanted to wait up.

He was asleep when I went into his bedroom. He had early mornings, most of the time getting up at four a.m. to get ready for the day. I didn't want to wake him. Standing there, staring at him on the bed, I wished he'd wake up on his own.

The moonlight graced the edges of the heavy furniture he'd come into when he bought the inn. Some other pieces he'd purchased to match the early 1900s style.

"Dae?" he whispered softly in the half-light. "Is something wrong?"

"Not now." I climbed into bed beside him and pulled up the blanket before I ended up on his shoulder. "Kevin, I wish you believed in seafolk. I'm afraid one of them may have killed Captain Lucky."

He sighed and pulled me close. "Let's pretend I do believe in seafolk. Tell me about it."

I snuggled closer and told him about my new encounter with Lilly.

"But there's also a human — Tovi's girlfriend — who could be involved in this," he said. "That could make more sense."

"Get up," I urged. "It's not sunrise yet. We could wait down by the pier for Tovi to leave. When he does, maybe you can see him as a merman."

He glanced at the clock. "It's already one-thirty, Dae. I have to be up at four."

"But don't you want to see Tovi so all of this makes sense to you?"

"Sure. I want to see a merman." He took a deep breath. "Let's go."

We took Kevin's good camera and two mugs of coffee. There was always coffee in a big urn on the sideboard near the kitchen. I also grabbed some fresh chocolate chip cookies for the vigil. It was good to have something to eat while waiting.

There was no one at the pier when we got there. I

was kind of hoping Lilly might harass me again, but no such luck. The moon was hazy overhead, probably a sign of storms on their way. We sat on the bench where Lilly and Cathi had been and waited.

"Wouldn't it be better if they don't see us?" Kevin asked.

"I don't think it really matters. If he comes this way to jump back in the water like his sister, you'll see him, and we'll take his picture."

He sipped his coffee. "Why do you think he'll come this way?"

"Because I think his human girlfriend might be Cathi Connor. I saw her go into her rental house with Lilly, but I didn't see her come out again. I think she might be in there with Tovi."

Since it was going to be a long wait, I told him about getting Trudy and Tim back together.

"She promised to be there for me if I get cold feet — which isn't going to happen."

Kevin smiled. "You never know. The question is — who will be there for me if I get cold feet?"

"I thought you said you knew what you wanted. Have you changed your mind?"

"No. But marriage is stressful. I might before it happens."

I stared at him, loving the lines of his handsome face in the moonlight. "Have you ever been married? I mean, you're kind of old to get married for the first time."

"I could say that about you too." He grinned. "But I'm too much of a gentleman."

"You're right. We're both mature. We should know exactly what we want. We shouldn't have the problem

Trudy and Tim are having."

"Have you thought about where you'd like to get married, if we do?"

"I have. I think sunrise on the beach would be nice. It can't be at the Blue Whale because you'd run yourself ragged trying to get everything ready. That doesn't sound like a good beginning to the honeymoon."

"Oh." He put his arm around me. "The honeymoon. I suppose we get one of those, even if we are elderly."

"We're not *that* old," I joked. "We should go somewhere with lots of antiques that I could buy for the shop."

"No business!" He kissed me. "I can't look at food either. Just you and me and a few days away."

"I found a new link to Grandma Eleanore today," I told him. "It might be what I'm looking for to bring her home."

I told him the story of how she and Gramps had eloped.

"Maybe that's what we need to do," he said. "Skip the big deal and go right for the important part."

"But everyone would be so disappointed. I don't have six brothers and sisters like Gramps did. I think he'd probably kill me if he didn't get to walk me down the aisle."

"Since that would be a bad start to our future relationship, I guess we'll stay here."

"What about your family? You said they live in Maryland, right? Are you going to invite them?"

"Probably. I only have my parents and one brother. I really don't know if they'll come down for a wedding or just send money."

"Money is good, especially if we know ahead of time so we don't have to buy food, champagne, or those stupid little party favors Trudy likes so much."

"Are you sure it's a good idea to bring your grandmother home, Dae?" he asked. "Horace seems really happy with MC. Isn't that going to screw up everything between them?"

I looked into his eyes that were luminous in the light. "I can't just leave her there, lost in time, if there's some way to bring her back. I don't know what will happen if I can do it, but what kind of granddaughter would I be not to try?"

"Certainly not the kind that I know." He kissed me again and smiled.

Yawning, I glanced at my watch. "I'm sorry. I shouldn't have bothered you with waiting out here for a merman. Tovi could've left while we were at your place. We're both going to be miserable tomorrow on one of the busiest days of the year in Duck. Maybe you should change your mind about marrying me. I'm obviously self-centered and don't care what happens to you. You could get pneumonia and die."

"Yes, at my advanced, unmarried age. You'd feel guilty then, I bet."

"For a while," I agreed. "But then I'd marry someone else. I'm still eligible, you know."

We laughed together at that scenario and then the sound of fast-moving footsteps came toward us from the house we were watching.

"It's him." I picked up the camera. "It's Tovi. He's headed back to sea."

Like an unerring missile moving toward its target, Tovi ran quickly for the pier and the salt water beside it. The waves pushed to the shore even in the small cove they'd chosen to anchor the gambling ship.

"I see him," Kevin said. "But he's got two legs. Are you sure he's the right one?"

"Yes, he's the merman. Look out!"

I lifted the camera for a picture and saw Tovi running straight at me. The last thing I saw before I fell into the water was his hand going up to block the shot.

After that, I was in the surf. It wasn't very deep off the short end of the pier. I wasn't worried about drowning since I'd learned how to swim when I was very young.

It took a minute to disengage from Tovi landing squarely on top of me. His large tail had a powerful thrust as he kicked hard to get into deeper water.

I clung to the camera strap, not knowing if there was a viable image of him becoming a merman or not. I guess he didn't know either and was trying to protect his secret.

Kevin was yelling for me when I surfaced a moment later. I was glad he hadn't jumped in after me—that would've been embarrassing for a hardened Banker like myself.

"It's okay." I came up sputtering and holding the camera. "I've still got it."

He reached out a hand down and helped me out of the water.

"I saw him change," Kevin was yelling as he hugged me. "At the last minute, as he took you with him, I saw his legs become a big, blue and gold tail. There are seafolk!"

"That's what I've been telling you." I grinned and kissed him.

"No. Real seafolk, Dae. I can't think of any way he could have faked that. It was real."

Kevin is normally a little on the jaded side. Probably from the life he's led. It was fun to see how excited he was about me being right.

"Of course there are seafolk. At least two of them. Now let's go back to the Blue Whale so I can change clothes. I hope the camera caught what you saw. Tess will be so excited."

I always kept a spare set of clothes at the inn. Sometimes I worked in the garden or helped in the kitchen and got my clothes messed up. I changed quickly into the old jeans and green top I kept there, excited to see what might prove the existence of another race of people. I took a moment to text Tess and then hurried into the kitchen.

"Did I get it?" I stood behind Kevin while he was at the computer.

"You got something, but it looks like all those newspaper pictures of aliens and werewolves. It's hard to tell what it is."

I studied the image and was disappointed. "I can tell it's him. There's his tail as he's pushing me into the water. I kept snapping."

"This is the only one with any image at all. Sorry. I don't think anyone but me and you are going to believe this is a merman."

"We could probably sell it to *The Globe* or *The Enquirer* anyway." I put my arms around his neck. "That's okay. At least you saw him. I don't need to convince anyone else."

"I know this is too little, too late," he said. "But I'm sorry for doubting you. It won't ever happen again. I don't care if you see a little green man or Bigfoot. If you say you saw it, I believe it."

I kissed him. "You should've known better. You know how the weird things in life like me."

"Then I guess I must be one of the weirdest things because I like you a lot."

We were in each other's arms when Tess came running into the Blue Whale. I was pretty sure that she was still wearing her night clothes, not to mention one sandal and one tennis shoe.

"Well? You saw him. Did you get a picture?" She tried to get her tangled gray hair out of her face as she spoke.

Kevin kissed me one more time. "I'm going to make breakfast."

I showed Tess the image on the computer. She made it larger and smaller, trying to tighten the image and focus more on Tovi.

She finally gave up, clapping her hand down hard on the desk. "Blast it. This looks like all those other grainy, shadowy pictures of things they say don't exist. What a disappointment."

"On the other hand, Kevin saw him change, so I've made a believer of him. And I found out Tovi has a human girlfriend. That's something."

"Yes. It is. Even if we have to convince the world one person at a time, we'll do it. This is exciting news. Do you think it relates to your captain being murdered?"

"I'm not sure. I don't see why Tovi would want to kill Captain Lucky. His sister, Lilly, is another story. That mermaid has an attitude problem. But even then, why would she bother?"

"But Lilly told us her brother killed Captain Lucky," Tess pointed out.

"I know. But I don't believe her."

We went to join Kevin at the kitchen table, drawn by the smell of bacon and biscuits.

I got a text that Chief Michaels was doing much better and they expected him to come home the next day. It could still be weeks or months until he was able to go back to work. But just having him home from the hospital was good news. I wondered if Gramps would be filling in all that time.

"We have to devise a trap to catch Tovi or Lilly," Tess said between bites of food. "I don't mean to harm them in any way, but I would like a chance to talk to them, maybe draw some blood, and take pictures."

"I don't see how you could trap them," I said. "Not in a way that wouldn't hurt them."

"I could probably come up with something," Kevin volunteered.

Tess was thrilled about the idea, but I was reluctant. I'd seen the movie *Splash*. I didn't think anything good could come from the plan.

Chapter Fifteen

Tess left right after breakfast. She said she'd be back to talk to Kevin about his plan to catch one of the seafolk.

As soon as she was gone, I launched into a hundred reasons why he shouldn't help her.

"You know how these science things end up." I helped him clear the kitchen table and said good morning to his staff as they came in. "You shouldn't help her with this."

"But this is the chance of a lifetime," he insisted as he got out the menu for the day to give his cooks. "If we don't find a way to document this, no one will ever believe it."

"And that's just as well." I covered his hand with

mine. "What good will it do to document it? Maybe inviting hundreds of people to come here with nets and cameras? People around the world will start hunting them, like they did big white sharks after *Jaws*. We can't let that happen."

"I think you're overstating the case."

"Remember you said it might not be a good idea to bring Grandma Eleanore from the past? I think this is much worse, Kevin. Just because we know doesn't mean everyone else needs to know."

"I think these are two distinctly different ideas." He signed for his delivery of fresh flowers that would enliven the inn that day. "Look. I can't do anything today. Let's think about it and talk again tonight. If you really feel this would be bad, I won't do it."

That was a relief. "Thanks."

"And you won't keep trying to bring your grandmother back, because I think that's a really bad idea too."

"Kevin!"

"Later, sweetheart." He kissed my cheek. "I have to get breakfast going for my starving guests."

Now I was sorry I'd found a way to convince him that seafolk existed.

Angry and worried, I saw Mark Samson next door at the Duck Historical Museum. It was too early for him to be opening, but if he was there, maybe I could do some research.

"Hello!" I stuck my head in the open doorway. "Mark? Are you in here?"

"Good morning, Dae." He grinned as he put on a pot of coffee. "We have our monthly meeting this morning. I know—awful time for it, right? It's my turn to set up. Can you stay?"

I was officially on the board of the historical society but rarely attended meetings. I knew I should be more consistent, but I had to attend so many meetings as mayor that the idea of one more set my teeth on edge. I loved our historical society and had used it many times for reference. But the meetings were very dry, and Mrs. Euly Stanley tended to be long-winded.

"Could I just do a little digging? Something has come up, and I'd like to take a look at the back issues of the *Duck Gazette*, and anything else that pertains to my investigation."

"Your investigation, huh? Sounds fun. I must need a new job." He shook his head. "I think cooking ribs must be getting to me if I think your job is exciting!"

I didn't ask him what he meant by that.

The *Duck Gazette* had been the original newspaper for the town. It had been gone for many years, but the historical society kept it alive with microfiche. Anyone could still view the old pictures and stories, including information about the Blue Whale and its original owner, Bunk Whitley. A lot of Duck folklore would have been lost if it wasn't for the museum and the newspaper archives.

"You're looking for stuff about mermaids, aren't you?" Mark grinned. "I'm sure everyone will be. Good thing we're having a meeting today so we can discuss how to handle the crowds we can expect."

"Wait. What?" I walked past the lifelike statue of my ancestor, Rafe Masterson, the Scourge of Duck. "Why would you think I'd be looking for information about mermaids?"

"I don't know. Maybe this morning's copy of *Duck*

Aloud?" He held up the newspaper. There was a huge headline — Mermaid Spotted in Duck — with a picture of Tovi.

Without meaning to, I snatched it from him and stared at the picture. It was grainy and might or might not have been a merman at all. I could make out his face and the shock of black hair on his head. There was clearly a curve to his hips and tail.

I knew most people would laugh at it, but many others would take it for gospel. No doubt it had already hit the Internet.

"Sorry." I gave the copy back to him with a sheepish smile. "I was stunned."

"That's okay. I felt the same way when I saw it. I bought a bunch of copies and put them over there if you want to take one." He looked at the picture too. "Manfred Vorst may have hit the jackpot this time. But look at the name under the picture."

My eyes went to the caption. *Photo by Captain William Lucky.* That was even weirder.

"Thanks, Mark. I guess I'll come back for that research. I'm going to pay Mr. Vorst a call."

"See you later, Dae."

I stalked quickly through yards and down side paths to avoid the crowded roads. Were there already thousands more people in Duck? It seemed that way to me. I had no cell phone service on my way to Manfred's tiny office in an outbuilding in his yard, but I had a feeling the information was already on YouTube.

Manfred was in his office when I arrived. He was on his cell phone with one hand and his landline with the other. I could tell from the way he was speaking that he was very excited about his latest work.

I looked at the *Duck Aloud* website pulled up on his computer. Not only did Manfred have the grainy picture posted, there was a video that went with it. I wondered if the video included Cathi Connor.

"Mayor O'Donnell!" He greeted me effusively. "It's a wonderful day, isn't it? No pun intended on your name. What can I do for you?"

"You can take down these pictures and tell me why you put Captain Lucky's name on them."

I had barely said the words when Officer Scott Randall drove up with Sheriff Riley coming in right after him.

"I've got some questions for you, Vorst," Sheriff Riley said. "Let's start with why you killed Captain Lucky to steal these pictures from him."

Everyone started talking at once. Sheriff Riley accused Manfred of killing Captain Lucky to get the merman picture and video. Manfred started explaining why he hadn't killed Captain Lucky and how he'd bought the images from him before he died.

"I have the receipt right here." Manfred produced it with a flourish. "I even took a picture of it for authenticity with the time stamp on my camera. You don't have anything on me, unless you want to give me a medal for being a sharp business man."

"You should have told us about this when you heard Captain Lucky was dead," Sheriff Riley said.

"Oh. Is he dead?" Manfred managed to look surprised. "I've been so busy, you know. I can't keep up with everything."

Scott nodded. "Don't try to lie about it. I just saw the article about his death in your paper, Mr. Vorst. I think you know what happened to Captain Lucky."

"But that doesn't mean I participated in it," Manfred argued.

"Never mind that." Sheriff Riley stopped him. "You're coming with me to answer some questions."

"I'm sorry, Sheriff Riley," Scott said. "Chief O'Donnell said not to let you take him anywhere until we've questioned him."

The sheriff laughed. "This is my case as much as it is Horace's. I'll take him where I want. I don't think you're going to stop me, Officer Randall."

Had they all just lost their minds?

"Why not take him to the Duck Police Department to be interviewed, and then if he seems guilty of something, you can take him to Manteo, Sheriff Riley? You know we don't have a nice, big jail here like you do." I smiled sweetly as I intervened.

"You should interview Mayor O'Donnell while you're at it," Manfred said. "I know that Captain Lucky gave her a personal possession to hold for him. She could be as guilty of killing him as I am."

Sheriff Riley cuffed him, but he stared at me. "Is that true, Dae?"

How could I explain that the coral horn needed to be protected because it gave me a bad feeling in the pit of my stomach? How had Manfred known about it?

"He didn't give me anything of value. It's a big seashell. He told me he was going out of town and asked me to hang on to it until he got back." *Only a tiny lie.*

The sheriff glared and told Scott to bring me in too. Scott looked fairly alarmed at the idea, his brow furrowed and eyes wide, but I wasn't worried about it.

I could explain this to Gramps.

"It's okay," I told Scott. "I'm sure Sheriff Riley is only being thorough."

Manfred struggled with the sheriff. "This is against my constitutional rights. Let me go. I'll take this to the Supreme Court."

"Pipe down, Vorst." The sheriff shoved him into the back of his car. "Vermin like you were meant to be caught."

In contrast, Scott held the front passenger side door open for me. I got in, and he closed the door behind me. I definitely got the better of the two lawmen. But the result was going to be the same.

I hoped I'd hear if Captain Lucky actually sold those photos to Manfred. If he could prove there was a merman in Duck, why didn't he put them on the Internet himself?

But this supported my idea that Lilly could have murdered Captain Lucky, hoping to get the pictures. But Captain Lucky had already given them to Manfred. I needed more answers.

We drove to the new town hall, and Scott carefully helped me out of the car. Sheriff Riley jerked Manfred around like a fish on a line. We were a small parade going into the police department door with plenty of gawking faces following us.

"What's going on?" Gramps asked from behind the front desk. "Tuck, what are you up to?"

Sheriff Riley grabbed Gramps's arm and hauled him into Chief Michaels's office. I was surprised that Gramps hadn't taken that office already—it was the only one that had any privacy in the large room. Maybe he wasn't comfortable being in there since his job was only temporary.

Without much crime in Duck, we didn't need a larger space or a real jail. We sufficed with what we had until prisoners could be handed over to the sheriff's office, which was much larger and better staffed.

"You better come clean on what you know, Madam Mayor," Manfred warned. "I'm not taking the fall for this by myself."

I really didn't know what he was talking about. Besides holding on to the coral horn and not telling anyone about it, I wasn't guilty of anything. True, I knew about the seafolk — but that wasn't a crime either.

"Did you kill Captain Lucky to get that picture and video?" I asked him.

"No, of course not. He asked me to hold it in case something happened to him. I guess he was scared for a reason since he's dead now. Probably killed by one of these sea creatures, huh?"

Chapter Sixteen

"But why would anyone want to kill him because he could prove there were seafolk?"

"They didn't kill him for that, I'm sure," he retorted in a snarky tone of voice. "Why don't you pick up one of his belongings and give us all some answers?"

"That's enough prisoner fraternization." Sheriff Riley came out of the office.

"You're not a prisoner, Dae," Gramps said. "But I want to talk to you a minute, please."

"Don't get your hopes up. You're not going free," the sheriff said to Manfred. "I'm taking you back to Manteo for interrogation. Let's go."

"You got the wrong man." Manfred struggled and argued. "I didn't kill anyone."

The two of them got out the front door, and Scott sat heavily in his chair.

"I'm sorry, Mayor O'Donnell. And I'm glad they're gone. I can't believe Manfred killed Captain Lucky."

"He didn't," I assured him.

"Then who did? The seafolk?"

"I don't think it was them either."

"If you please, Dae." Gramps impatiently held the door open to the office.

I smiled at Scott and preceded Gramps into Chief Michaels's office.

He shut the door behind us. "What is this all about? Is this what you were trying to say about the naked man who accosted you?"

"Yes. There is a merman and a mermaid in Duck. But I don't think they killed Captain Lucky."

"Why not?"

"Because there was no reason for them to kill him. Tovi is the merman. He's very nice. Lilly isn't quite as nice, but I don't think she'd set Captain Lucky up on the ship that way, do you? What would be the point when she could just wrap her tail around him and drag him under the sea forever?"

"Damn it, Dae, you should have told me you were involved in some way!"

Gramps was more upset than I understood for him to swear at me.

"I'm really only involved in a minimal way because Captain Lucky gave me the coral horn that calls the seafolk before he died."

"That horn is evidence. Bring it in so we can take a look at it."

"No one can blow it, Gramps. I think that's what

brought Tovi and Lilly to us in the first place."

"Do I need to send Scott with you?"

"No. I'll bring it in."

"Dae?"

"I'll bring it in, Gramps." I glanced at his raised brow and annoyed expression. "The sooner Chief Michaels can take over again, the sooner I go back to not feeling like a teenager. You're not the sheriff anymore!"

I didn't slam the office door, but I was irritated at the way he'd treated me. He didn't even know what I had—just assumed it had something to do with the murder. I understood that he was under pressure to fill Chief Michaels's shoes, but he didn't have to take it out on me.

Scott nodded to me, and I left town hall.

The coral horn was still at Missing Pieces, but I wasn't going there until I had a chance to shower, get the saltwater off me, and change clothes. I knew if I went to the shop first, I had a good chance of not leaving again until late. Everyone would be buzzing about the merman picture. It was the way the town's grapevine worked.

Plus I'd promised Treasure that I'd bring him to the shop. There was also the matter of taking all the family goodies I'd found in the attic to fill in the holes that had been created by sales the day before.

Lucky for me that Gramps had Chief Michaels's police car and didn't need the golf cart. It would be a good way to transport everything to Missing Pieces.

I walked home quickly and wasn't happy to see someone waiting on the front steps for me. It wasn't a good time to talk about the future of Duck or why the water tower wasn't painted more frequently.

To my surprise, it was Cathi Connors.

"Can we talk?" she asked me.

"Sure. Let's go inside." I opened the front door, and she followed me in. I knew what she wanted to talk about.

"Dae, you have to put a stop to all this speculation about Tovi and Lilly. You know where this will lead. Both of us are history majors. Neither one of us wants to see new witch trials taking place in Duck—except with seafolk. It will be a freak show. Tovi and Lilly will be taken away and analyzed to death. You know it's true."

I sat opposite her at the kitchen table. "I agree with you. We can't let them be captured."

"About the photos and video—"

"There's nothing I can do about that. You know how the Internet is, Cathi. Once it gets out there, it's always there."

"Then it's too late to stop it."

"I won't release the picture I got of Tovi changing into a merman. Not that it was much to look at anyway. The one in the paper wasn't great either. This will all die down after a while. You can talk to Tovi. Tell him that he and his sister need to stay away from Duck for a while."

She got to her feet and paced the worn wood floor. "It's not that easy. He feels like he has as much right to be here as we do."

"I'm sure that's true. I know he thinks he knows all about humans, but he's wrong. Explain it to him, graphically, if you need to."

"I'll try again."

"He doesn't want to leave because he's in love with you, isn't he?"

"What?" She seemed puzzled. "No. I'm just friends with both of them. I have been for years. He's in love with a human, but I don't know who it is. Lilly just wants to protect him from us and their elders."

"Did she kill Captain Lucky to keep him from posting those pictures?"

"No. Absolutely not! Tovi and Lilly told me about the pictures. They threatened Captain Lucky, but they didn't kill him. They aren't like that, Dae."

I looked at her red eyes and pale face. "How did you get involved with them?"

She smiled. "I was down by the water—this was years ago, after the divorce. I was thinking about jumping in and never coming back. I was so lonely, Dae. I just couldn't stand it."

"I'm so sorry, Cathi."

"Don't be. It led me to Tovi and Lilly. They suddenly appeared in the water. Tovi was lonely too. We tried being together, but he was looking for someone else, despite the rules of his people and the stupidity of mine. But it doesn't matter. I'm happy for the first time in years. I don't want anything or anyone to take that away."

Her eyes were fierce when she stared at me. I'd known Cathi all my life. She always seemed so strong and capable. I wondered if she really still loved Tovi but was content being his friend while he looked for the other woman. That didn't sound like a happy ending.

"What will they do? With the newspaper article and the Internet, they'll have to go away or risk being captured."

"I've thought about it," she said. "I don't think they'll be here much longer. You know they say seafolk are born from drowning victims. I'd be willing to die to this world, Dae, to be with them in the next. I hope they take me with them."

"You don't mean that. Think about what you're saying."

"I have—a lot. If they'll take me, I'll go." She smiled and hugged me. "So don't get everyone all riled up looking for me if I disappear. Just know that I'm happy and with them."

"Cathi—"

"See you later, Dae."

I watched her leave the house, torn between trying to find help for her before she did something she couldn't come back from and minding my own business. Was it was true that mermaids were drowning victims? I'd heard it all my life. I knew Cathi had too. But neither one of us could swear to it.

On the other hand, I wasn't in love with a merman. Maybe I'd be willing to take my chances if Kevin was a merman.

The desperate tone of her voice started me thinking. Was it possible Cathi had killed Captain Lucky? She obviously felt passionately about protecting Tovi and Lilly. It would explain the human touch I thought had been responsible for hitting him in the head.

With a sigh, I went upstairs and played with Treasure for a while. He was so happy to see me. I was sure he thought I'd forgotten about taking him to the shop. I hadn't seen Baylor anywhere, but he was probably with Mary Catherine.

I asked Treasure if he wouldn't rather stay at home where he could enjoy his privacy, but he went over and pawed at the special tote bag I'd made to carry him. That was good enough for me.

Thinking about Cathi and Tovi, I got dressed in clean pink shorts and a tank top with the summer Duck logo on it. Who was I to stop Cathi if this was really what she wanted? My mood was contemplative as I took everything I'd scavenged from the attic out to the golf cart.

Love was something different for everyone. I hoped Cathi wouldn't end up going away with Tovi, but I wasn't going to try to stop her. Captain Lucky's murder was another matter. If I found that Cathi had killed him, it wouldn't be right to let her swim away with no responsibility.

I was down to the last two pieces I'd found in the attic—Gramps's wedding memento and my mother's souvenirs from her day at the carnival with a psychic. I didn't plan to sell either of these and tucked my mother's souvenir into the drawer of my bedside table. The case that held Grandma Eleanore's pink garter was pretty in an old fashioned way. I picked it up to admire it, almost feeling her personal essence from it.

But as soon as I touched it, there was a sharp zap, like from an electrical outlet or an appliance with wiring problems. I pulled back from it and let the garter fall to the floor. There was a bright red welt on my finger. That had never happened to me before.

Treasure stuck his nose in the garter as he examined it. He sniffed it a few times and then walked away toward the bag I used to carry him.

"Okay. I get it. I'm ready to go. We'll have to take

this stuff to Missing Pieces and then take the coral horn to Gramps. I hope you're up for some travel."

He meowed and rubbed up against my bare legs. I laughed and put him in the bag. He was usually good in there when I carried him places with me. Fortunately he wasn't the size of Baylor, or I wasn't sure if I'd be able to carry him. I couldn't figure out how Mary Catherine could balance that enormous cat around her neck without slumping forward.

"I guess it happened with practice," I told Treasure who purred in understanding.

I scooped up the garter from the floor and put it in the drawer. Kevin's strong words of caution regarding Grandma Eleanore rang in my ears from that morning. But could I just let it go the way he wanted me to and not bring Grandma Eleanore home if it was possible? It wasn't like I was bringing her back from the dead after all—she'd never really died—just had become lost in time.

There was a noise from downstairs. I thought it was probably Gramps on break and looking around for cookies to go with his coffee. I went down, hoping he wasn't still frowning as he had been at the police department.

I froze halfway down the stairs as I heard singing. With my heart racing and knees trembling, I went slowly down the rest of the stairs until I could see into the kitchen.

"There you are," Grandma Eleanore said in her cheerful voice. "Come down and have some tea with me. It's seems we have a lot to talk about."

Chapter Seventeen

"How did you get here?"

My words were slow and hesitant. I was excited and scared at the same time. I wanted to hug her and cry. Was she real, or a ghost of the past I'd brought forward?

"Is that all you can say?" She came quickly toward me and took me in her arms. "Oh my Lord, how I've wanted to do that. My beautiful Dae. It's so good to be home."

I stood completely still for about five seconds before I put my arms around her and hugged with all my might. "How is this possible? I didn't do anything."

"Sometimes it's not how hard you work at something—it's doing exactly the right thing." She left one arm around my waist, and we walked into the kitchen. "With our gift, it's a matter of finding exactly the right item or person to see what we need. What did you recently find that belonged to me?"

"I found the stuff from your and Gramps's honeymoon in Wilmington. I was just looking at it after I opened the case that held your garter." I stuck out my finger and showed her where it had zapped me. "What was that?"

"My grandmother, who passed the gift to me, called it life spark. What she meant was finding the thing you needed to do to follow your heart."

"I can't believe it. I thought it would be more complicated."

Grandma Eleanore reminded me so much of my mother, except rounder and softer. Their faces were so much alike. My mother had come to wear a lot of unhappy lines around her eyes and mouth before she died. My grandmother appeared to have avoided that kind of unhappiness in her life.

"I wouldn't have thought my garter would be the key." She shrugged. "But it's always a missing piece of our lives that frees us or holds us back."

"I'm glad you're not angry that I kept trying." I smiled. "Once Gramps told me that you weren't dead—you just never came back—I couldn't stop thinking about it. *Gramps*! I have to call him."

I pulled out my cell phone, and she stared at it.

"I can see I have a lot of catching up to do," she said. "You actually carry a phone around in your pocket now?"

"Not just a phone," I explained as I punched in Gramps's number. "It's information from all over the world. News and music. You can call or send messages to a person in China if you want to."

"That's amazing."

"O'Donnell," Gramps barked his name impatiently.

"You have to come home right now," I said. "You won't believe what's happened."

"Dae, I don't have time to play games. I'm out at the Andalusia. Did you take that thing Captain Lucky gave you to the police department yet?"

"It doesn't matter." I wiped tears from my face and eyes. "None of it matters right now. Come home, Gramps. Don't do anything else. Just come home."

"What's wrong?" His tone changed abruptly. "Are you in trouble? Are you hurt?"

"Please, Gramps. Come home now."

"I'll be there in five minutes."

I sat down, trying to imagine the impact this would have on him. His life would be completely different now too.

The front door opened. It was Mary Catherine, with Baylor wrapped around her neck and shoulders like a shawl, almost matching her hair.

"Hello, Dae." Her inquisitive green eyes went to my grandmother. "I don't think we've met. Mary Catherine Roberts." She held out her hand, and Baylor lifted his big head.

"Eleanore O'Donnell."

Mary Catherine, stunned, sat in a kitchen chair beside me. "You did it. You really did it. You brought her back."

"I know." I knew it would have a big impact on Mary Catherine as well. "Gramps is on his way home."

"I would imagine so."

"Would you like some tea?" Grandma Eleanore asked her. "You know, it feels like I just woke up here this morning. I can see there have been a few changes, but it's as though they happened while I was sleeping."

"Is this the way everything was the day you disappeared?" I asked. "Are you the same age?"

"As far as I can tell," she answered. "It's a little mixed up for me right now."

"I believe I need something stronger than tea," Mary Catherine said. "How did you do this, Dae? Time can't change, and people can't swim through it like we do through water."

"You know about Dae's gift," Grandma Eleanore said. "You walked in without knocking. Are you living here? Are you married to Horace now?"

I heard the screech of tires as Gramps turned sharply into the drive from Duck Road.

"No," Mary Catherine assured her. "I'm not married to Horace. I'm just…a friend of the family. Dae was nice enough to invite me to stay until I could decide if I should live in Duck permanently."

Grandma Eleanore smiled at me. "I always knew that's how she'd be."

Gramps burst through the front door with his gun drawn.

"What's going on?" he demanded. "Are you hurt, Dae?"

"Horace!" Grandma Eleanore scolded. "Have things changed so much that you'd come in here with your gun in your hand?"

I thought Gramps might fall to the floor. The look of shock on his face when he saw her was so powerful. His mouth hung open, and his eyes bulged. The hand that held his sidearm dropped, and he staggered forward.

"Eleanore? Is that *really* you?"

"It's really me, Horace. Our granddaughter brought me back."

She ran to him and hugged him, scattering kisses on his face like raindrops during a storm. They were so close that nothing could have come between them.

He put his hands on her shoulders and touched her arms. "I don't understand. How could this happen? It's been so long. I never thought I'd see you again."

Their lips met and clung. They were both crying as they touched each other's faces and spoke their names in sweet whispers.

Mary Catherine and I were both crying too. I hugged her as we stood together watching this miracle happen.

"This can't happen," Mary Catherine said as she wiped her eyes. "It's against the laws of nature."

"She's right here. I think the laws of nature may be a little bent in Duck, just not broken."

She shook her head and slowly walked outside. Baylor followed at her feet.

Treasure peeked out of his bag, wondering what was happening and why we hadn't left.

"Let's sit down a minute," Gramps said. "A lot has happened while you were gone."

"I'm a little up to date, thanks to Dae's regular visits." She took his hand. "I know Jean is gone."

"Yes." He swallowed hard. "It was a hard time to get through."

I could see I was unnecessary at that moment. "I'm going to Missing Pieces to get the coral horn Chief

O'Donnell wants to see. Maybe you could drop Grandma Eleanore off at the shop when you go back to work."

"Don't leave," she said. "Stay a while."

"You two have things to say that you don't need an audience for. I'll see you soon." I hugged her hard before I left. "I love you. We won't be apart for long. I have a million things I want to talk to you about."

I picked up my bag and went out to the golf cart. Mary Catherine was waiting there.

"You must've guessed that I'm on my way to Missing Pieces." I stowed my cat bag behind me. Treasure stared at Baylor sitting on the seat above him, but didn't come out.

"Yes. Do you mind if I ride along?"

"No. Not at all." I wiped my eyes one last time and sniffed. "I had no idea this was going to happen, especially not this way. I didn't know what to expect."

Her green eyes were focused on me as I backed the golf cart down the drive to Duck Road.

"Whatever you did, Dae, I don't know if it can stand. All my instincts tell me this is wrong."

"You too?" I shook my head. "Kevin pretty much said the same thing. You know, she wasn't dead. Our gift allows us to go back in time when we touch something. I didn't know that until recently, even though I was doing it. I didn't resurrect her. I just kind of wished her home."

"Correct me if I'm wrong, but when did the laws of time become mutable? When you go back to visit a time and place where an object you're investigating came from, you don't stay, and you don't bring anything or anyone back with you. You're only there a short while, and then you come back."

"That's different. Grandma Eleanore wasn't from the time she got trapped in."

"She's not from this time either, Dae. She's been gone for forty years."

I didn't want to hear anything bad about Grandma Eleanore being back. It was a blessing, a miracle. Why couldn't she see that?

"You know, our relationship won't change. And you're still welcome to stay at the house. You don't have to worry about not being part of our lives. It won't be that way."

We were at the Duck Shoppes, parked as close to the loading ramp as I could get. I could have driven the golf cart right up to Missing Pieces, but people frowned on driving across the boardwalk.

Mary Catherine smiled and hugged me. "I'm sure it will be all right, Dae. Do you want some help taking these things to your shop?"

I let her help me take some stuff. Even with our two loads, I was going to have to make another trip. The old clocks were heavy. We talked the whole way to the shop.

"Are we seriously thinking that the seafolk murdered Captain Lucky?" she asked.

"No. I don't think Gramps or Sheriff Riley want to think that at all." I laughed. "That would mean admitting that there are seafolk. Neither one of them want to do that."

"What about you?" she asked as I opened the shop door. "Do you think Lilly or Tovi murdered him?"

"I don't think so. There are a few human suspects." I told her about Cathi, Manfred, and whoever Tovi was in love with. "It makes more sense for a human to have killed him, Mary Catherine. But I don't know which one. Kevin and Tess want to trap one of the seafolk."

"That can't be allowed to happen. What is Kevin thinking?"

"He wants to prove they exist. I think he's still in shock because I proved it to him. I hope he comes to his senses. Tess just wants to know what makes them tick. She's searched for them her whole life."

She put down the two clocks she was holding. "I understand that. But if you need help to keep it from happening, Dae, tell me. We both know what it would be like if this was proven to the entire world."

"Yes. We're on the same page with that." I hugged her again and thanked her for her help. "And don't worry about Grandma Eleanore. Everything will be fine. Things have gone back to the way they should be."

"I'm sure you're right." She glanced at the floor. "Come on, Baylor. Let's not stand around all day."

Her feelings were hurt. I knew it would be hard on her to have my grandmother back. She and Gramps had such a good relationship. That was over now. I had to find a way to make sure she knew she would still be part of our lives.

I'd managed to bring Treasure up with me. He crawled out of his cat bag as soon as Baylor was gone. I quickly closed the front door — or at least tried to — closing it instead on Mrs. Euly Stanley.

"I'm so sorry." I opened it quickly. "I hope you're not hurt."

Mrs. Stanley looked fragile and old, but she was tough. She brushed off her green dress and straightened the cute straw hat she was wearing on her white hair.

"Don't fuss, Dae. I'm fine. I hoped I'd find you here. I heard you were researching mermaids at the museum as the news broke that we have two of them with us right now."

"That's true. Would you like a cup of tea?"

"I'd rather have a small glass of Jack Daniels, but I doubt you have it, so tea will suffice. Thank you."

We sat down together on the burgundy brocade sofa, and I remembered her diamond ring that I'd found. I gave it to her, and she sniffed.

"Where in the world did you find this?" She wiped a tear from her eye. "I thought it was lost forever. But that's what you do, isn't it? A finder of lost things. Just like Eleanore and her grandmother before her. Thank you, Dae. I will treasure it. This ring brings back so many good memories of my husband, David. He's been gone so long."

Treasure meowed when he thought he'd heard his name, but darted under my chair to stare at our guest.

"What can I do for you, Mrs. Stanley?"

"I'm here about the seafolk, Dae. I have a story to tell you."

Chapter Eighteen

I had never thought of Mrs. Stanley as the storytelling sort. She tended to be a little sharp around the edges, impatient, and just not the type to share life tales.

Maybe it was because I'd found her engagement ring. Maybe it was the warm weather. Whatever it was, she sat back against the sofa, her eyes becoming misty with the past.

"It was my sixteenth summer. I was disappointed because my mother wouldn't allow me to go with my friend, Stephanie, to a week-long college orientation at Eastern Carolina College. She said my friends were rowdy and there weren't enough adult chaperones. I was furious with her and spent most of that week at the beach by myself."

I sipped my tea and tried to imagine her as a wild teenager. My imagination wasn't that good.

"I got up very early each morning and slipped out. I stayed out past my curfew. I dared my mother to say anything after she had treated me so unfairly. My mother, being a wise and sensitive woman, said nothing. So I found myself at the beach one evening as it was getting dark. I was staring at the horizon when I saw a man come out of the water."

Treasure butted his head against me for attention, and I scratched behind his ears.

"It seemed as though he was floating in with the waves until he reached the shore and got up on his feet." She giggled and put her hand over her mouth. "He was completely naked. Can you imagine?"

"Well—"

"Of course nowadays it's nothing. But back then, people were appropriately clothed at all times." She smiled and returned to her reminiscing. "It was the first time I had ever seen a naked body besides my own. Even then, I was careful not to look in the mirror as I got out of the tub. No good can ever come from that."

It was my turn to hide my smile.

"But there he was—tall, handsome and very well-endowed—though I didn't know it at the time. He walked right over to me. I couldn't move. I was beyond amazement seeing him there. He started talking and asked me my name. He said he lived in the water, but sometimes he came to the land and could walk around on legs until sunrise the next day."

So Mrs. Euly Stanley had seen a merman. That was

something I hadn't considered.

"What did you do?" I asked.

"Oh we met there every evening after that until the end of summer vacation. We talked — he told the most amazing stories. His eyes moved, as though there was water inside them, ebbing and flowing like the tide. They changed color as he moved. I've never seen anything like it again. I told him about myself. We talked about my life. I was sure I was in love with him, and he professed his love for me."

I sat on the edge of the seat, last sip of tea forgotten.

"But he told me humans weren't allowed to be with his kind. I would have to drown and come back to be with him." She sighed. "Even then I was too practical to believe such a thing was possible. I told him no thanks and asked if there was any way he could become a human and we could be married. He said that couldn't happen and that he had already been human once a hundred years before."

"So you had to let him go."

"Yes. Sometimes I still dream about him. I wonder now if I could find him if he'd still like to be with me. I might consider his proposal."

"But you shared a kiss?" I asked with a smile.

"Good heavens no! Stephanie had known a girl who got pregnant from kissing her boyfriend. I wouldn't let that happen, although we did hug a bit."

I didn't say anything for a few minutes, marveling that she had chosen to share that story with me.

Finally she continued. "But that is why the seafolk must be left alone to live their lives around us. We can't allow one of them to be captured, or the entire race could be destroyed. I don't want to think about my merman being experimented on."

"I understand. I feel the same way."

She got slowly to her feet. "I'd wager that handsome Captain Lucky was messing around with something he shouldn't have been, and that's what killed him, not a merman. Good morning to you. Please say hello to your grandfather and tell him that we appreciate him taking Chief Michaels's job during this time."

"Thank you. I will."

It was hard for me to believe that the stalwart, very proper, respectful Mrs. Euly Stanley had once hugged a merman! That was a story that should be in the archives, though I doubted it ever would be.

I hurried back down to the golf cart to retrieve the last of my items and came back to Missing Pieces. For a long time, I stood next to the rail on the boardwalk and looked out over the Currituck Sound.

It was fascinating to think about the seafolk out there living in the water. I was glad to hear that Mrs. Stanley was a believer too. I knew there couldn't be many of us without causing problems for them, but I was glad I was one of those who knew the truth.

The next hour passed quickly as I shined up the clocks and carefully set everything I'd brought in my best sales locations. There was an old necklace that I'd brought with me—just made of string and blue glass beads. But every time I looked at it, I had the urge to hold it and see exactly who it had belonged to. It kept calling to me, my eyes straying to it as I moved around the shop.

I was about to indulge my curiosity when Gramps and Grandma Eleanore walked in.

"Could I see you outside here for a minute, Dae?" Gramps asked.

"Sure." I smiled at Grandma Eleanore. "I'll be right back. Take a look around. I'll give you a good deal on anything you like."

She laughed. Gramps and I went out on the boardwalk.

"What's up?" I asked him.

"I don't know if this occurred to you, but your grandmother is legally dead." He stared out over the water. "I had to do something when she didn't come back. Everyone thought she took the boat out and fell overboard. After ten years, she was declared dead."

"I guess. I didn't think about legal complications."

"We can say she found her way home, I suppose, but she looks exactly as she did the day she disappeared. I've aged, and the people who knew her have aged too. Some of her friends may recognize her."

"Well—there's no accounting for the benefits of good skin and genes, right?"

He smiled at me. "I'm so blown away by this, honey. I can hardly think. But I have to go to work. Stay with her. Don't let her wander off by herself. We don't know yet how this will affect her."

"I guess I'll just introduce her as my grandmother and let the chips fall where they may." I shrugged. "I'll have her with me all day. Do you still want the coral horn that Captain Lucky left with me?"

"Yes. Sorry. I know you don't think it could have anything to do with his death, but we can't take that chance. I'll make sure it's returned to you."

We went back inside, and I got the horn.

"This is it?" he asked as I handed it to him.

"I told you. Captain Lucky said it can call the seafolk. It makes a strange sound when you blow into it."

"I'll make sure no one does that. We don't need any more mermaid stories." He smiled at Grandma Eleanore. "I'm going to leave you with Dae, sweetheart. I'll see you later."

They kissed, and I smiled. This was the way it was supposed to be. Mary Catherine was wrong about the natural order of things.

When Gramps was gone, Grandma Eleanore sat on the sofa.

"You have amassed a considerable amount of missing pieces, Dae. I think some of them may have come from our attic."

"That's true," I admitted. "Would you like some tea?"

"No, I'm fine. What's going on that has your grandfather in such a dither?"

I explained about Captain Lucky's murder and showed her the picture of Tovi on the front page of the paper. "They've arrested Manfred Vorst, the new newspaper owner, for killing Captain Lucky, but I don't think it was him. We'll have to see as more information becomes available."

Grandma Eleanore's blue eyes were confused. "Are you the mayor, run the shop, and work as a police officer with your grandfather?"

"No. I'm not that ambitious. I get involved sometimes when I know the people things are happening to. Or in this case, the merman. There's something I'd like you to look at. It's been bothering me all morning. I pulled it out of the attic and cleaned it up. Do you know who it belonged to?"

I showed her the necklace with the blue glass beads.

"That belonged to your mother. I'm surprised it wasn't with her things. No wonder you were attracted to it. Have you tried going back to the carnival on the day she met with the psychic?"

"No. Not yet. I will." I hastened to assure her. "I've just been really busy."

"Why didn't you touch this yourself and find out where it came from?" She handed me the necklace. "Have you stopped doing that?"

"I haven't stopped—I'm just more wary. I had some really bad experiences. The whole fainting thing can be really embarrassing and hard to explain. I try to limit those occasions to when Gramps or Kevin are around."

"Kevin?" She smiled. "Is that a special man in your life?"

"Yes. Don't you remember that I told you about him one of the times that we met in the past?"

"I'm afraid my memory isn't what it once was. But I'd certainly love to meet Kevin."

"He may stop by for lunch." I wasn't looking forward to telling him what I'd done. I was sure his opinion would be the same as Mary Catherine's.

"That would be wonderful. I'm so impressed with how much Duck has grown while I've been gone. It's become a little city but so carefully planned. You and the town council should be proud of yourselves."

Some customers came in, and I tended to them. They bought a few items—nothing really fancy or expensive but not cheap souvenirs either. It wasn't a bad sale for the first one of the day.

Between customers, Grandma Eleanore and I talked about everything. She told me about her childhood, and I told her about mine with Gramps as Dare County Sheriff. I told her about my father who hadn't stayed with my mother because Gramps had scared him away. She told me about their courtship and her father's belief that Horace O'Donnell would never amount to anything.

"Fathers are like that," she said. "I know Horace can be a bit strict, but he has a good heart. And he believes in your gift. He always believed what I told him about things too. He was the only one. My mother thought my grandmother was crazy. When I was very young, we were forbidden to have contact with her. As soon as I was able, I used to sneak off to her house, and we talked about finding things. Our gift is not always an easy thing to live with."

"I got lucky with Kevin like that too. Except for mermaids, he always believes me when I tell him what I've seen. He believes me about mermaids now too. He swears he'll always believe me."

"When are you thinking about being married?"

Another customer came in and bought both of my antique clocks. I was so excited. Not having to pay anyone for the item meant pure profit for me. My shopkeeper's heart was thrilled.

As I was wrapping and bagging the clocks for my customer, Kevin showed up. He took one look at Grandma Eleanore, and I could tell from the expression on his face that he knew what had happened.

She made it official when he introduced himself.

"I'm Kevin Brickman, Dae's fiancé."

"Very nice to meet you. I'm Eleanore O'Donnell. Dae's grandmother."

He glanced back at me, sadness in his eyes. "I know."

Chapter Nineteen

"It's a pleasure to meet you, Eleanore," he said. "I've heard a lot about you."

Kevin recovered quickly without appearing to be impolite, but I knew what he was thinking. I smiled at my departing customer and wished him a good day. It was almost noon. I suggested that we go to lunch.

"Oh! Is the Rib Shack still open? I'd love to eat there," Grandma Eleanore said.

"Sure." I glanced at Kevin. "We can go there. It may be a little crowded since this is Fourth of July weekend. But we can wait."

"I don't want to put you out," she said. "But I would love to eat lunch there. They used to make the best hushpuppies in the world. Does Mickey Samson still run the place?"

"No. He's retired," I told her. "I think Mark is his son. He runs it now, but I'm pretty sure nothing else has changed."

"Sounds good," Kevin agreed. "We can take the Blue Whale golf cart or yours, Dae."

"The Blue Whale Inn," Grandma Eleanore said. "That was such a nice place in its time. When old Bunk Whitley ran it, it was the place to be. It got kind of run down after he left. Is it still open?"

"Kevin owns it now," I explained as I locked up Missing Pieces and we started down the sunlit boardwalk. "He does a great job with it. I'm sure we'll go there later."

"What a treat," she remarked.

We were walking past August Grandin on our way to the parking lot. He stopped dead in his tracks and stared at us as though he'd seen a ghost.

"Eleanore? Is that really you?"

"August." They hugged. "It's been so long."

"Is there a plan for this?" Kevin whispered as we stood off to the side.

"It doesn't matter," I said softly. "She was lost at sea. Now she's back. Everyone will deal with it."

"I'm sure you're right."

I glared at him, not liking his tone.

Grandma Eleanore and August were crying and trying to catch up while dozens of people had to walk around them. When they were finished, we started again for the parking lot. August had been very emotional seeing her but also had dozens of questions she couldn't answer.

"You know, I almost married him," she told us as we went down the stairs. "Your grandfather, bless his heart, was reluctant to pop the question. I was afraid he might never ask."

My golf cart was completely surrounded by a dozen other carts in the parking lot. Kevin's was in the clear, so we took his to the Rib Shack.

I sat in the back since the front was easier to get into for my grandmother. I really didn't want to discuss this with Kevin either. He was going to get snarky about me bringing Grandma Eleanore back. He wouldn't understand that I hadn't really meant to do it, not right now anyway.

The Rib Shack was crowded. Kevin managed to find a small space near the dumpster to park. Mark had been after the city for years to let him buy a piece of open property where a beach store had once been so he could convert it into more parking. But Chris Slayton's zoning plans didn't allow for bigger parking areas for a business directly on the sound. He was trying to keep that property for future town plans to create another beach access.

There was a line of people waiting to get inside as the smell of barbecue ribs, chicken, and pulled pork overwhelmed the scent of anything else. Inside, there were huge posters on the wall that Mark and his father had collected. Some of them were from the old racing circuit that was once lively in the area.

There was a huge picture of Mad Dog on the wall with his winning race car. Beside him was Lightning Joe Walsh, another very popular driver who had something in common with Grandma Eleanore—he'd vanished for many years before we'd found his body as we were building the new Duck Town Hall.

"Mayor!" Luke Helms, the District Attorney for Dare County, was sitting at a big table. He called us over to share it with him.

He and Kevin shook hands as the waiter seated us. I introduced Grandma Eleanore with no problem. Luke had only lived in Duck for a short while. He didn't know many of our older secrets.

"You must be visiting," he remarked to her with a grin on his handsome face and a big plate of ribs in front of him on the wood table.

"Oh no. I'm originally from Duck." She glanced at me, catching on to the situation. "But I've been living out of town for a while."

"Eleanore O'Donnell! I thought that was you. When did you get back?" Mark's father, Mickey, joined us, pushing in another chair at the table. "My God! You look just like you did forty years ago when you disappeared."

"Forty years?" Luke smiled at me. "She's been gone a while."

"She was in an accident," I confided. "They thought she was dead. But here she is, back after all those years."

"That's a fantastic story. Almost as good as the merman killing Captain Lucky." Luke took a sip of his sweet tea. "I like Vorst for it. Makes more sense. I've lived here a couple of years, but I've never seen a mermaid."

"That doesn't mean they don't exist," Kevin said. "I don't know about you, but I've become more open to possibilities since I came to live in Duck."

Luke nodded. "That's because you've been dating

Dae."

Mickey Samson went to get his beer from another table and brought a second visitor back with him.

"Eleanore!" Mad Dog pushed Mickey aside to hug her. "How is this possible? We had a funeral for you, the biggest one this town has ever seen. When did you get back? Why hasn't Horace told anyone?"

"And the mystery thickens," Luke said. "You didn't say everyone thought she was dead, Mayor. That's not exactly a disappearance. Where is Chief O'Donnell anyway? Does he know his wife is back in town?"

We finally were able to order lunch. The crowd was stifling, even though I could hear the large air conditioning units buzzing close to the window where we were seated. Mad Dog's voice boomed over the loud music until I felt that everyone in Duck would know about Grandma Eleanore being back in the next hour or so.

I was tightly pushed next to Kevin, who was in the corner by the wall. So many people had stopped by the table that I could hardly see or hear my grandmother. I wasn't sure this was what Gramps had in mind when he'd said we should lay low for a while.

"There's no way to adequately explain this," Kevin hinted quietly near my ear. "Your grandparents are going to be overwhelmed with it."

"It will pass," I told him stiffly. "Don't always assume the worst."

"I thought you were going to stop pursuing this."

"I didn't say that—not that it matters. I didn't have any idea that this would happen when I woke up this morning. I had some old information from their wedding. I went downstairs, and there she was."

"You can't pull someone out of time, Dae. It won't work. It was different for you to go back. She won't be able to stay here."

I turned to stare angrily into his concerned eyes. "You aren't a specialist on what's possible with time, or with our gift, as far as I know. No one knows what's possible, Kevin. Don't lecture me. She's back, and it's a good thing."

He didn't say another word as we finished lunch, despite the crowds that came by to gawk at Grandma Eleanore and ask her uncomfortable questions about where she'd been. He took us back to the Duck Shoppes when lunch was over and invited her to visit the Blue Whale.

I watched him drive away with some regret that I'd allowed things to become angry between us, but he didn't understand how important this was to me and Gramps. He'd never lost someone in his family and not been able to find them again, never knowing what had happened to them.

"Are you fighting with your young man because of me?" Grandma Eleanore asked as we went back to Missing Pieces.

"No. Not exactly. We'll get over it. You know how it is. Couples fight. We'll be fine."

She held my hand as we walked past the Currituck Sound. "I never really thought I'd be back here with you and Horace. Thank you for this, Dae. I love you."

"I love you too." I squeezed her hand. "Now let's get busy. I want to know everything you know about our gift. You can't imagine what it was like being raised by Mom and Gramps. They tried not to look at me like I had two heads all the time—but it was hard for them."

She laughed. "I was raised very similarly since my mother only allowed me to have limited time with my grandmother. And after I'd heard her referred to as that 'crazy old woman' more than a few times, I was very careful about what I said to my parents."

There were UPS packages for me at the door. I gave Treasure a treat when we went inside Missing Pieces. And that was the last sane moment we spent at the shop that day.

It was unfortunate that it wasn't because I had a ton of paying customers. Instead, the shop was jammed with people who knew my grandmother or had heard the new gossip related to her. Everyone came— including Manfred Vorst with his cell phone camera.

"Surprised to see me, Madam Mayor?" He looked pleased by the idea that I didn't want him there.

"Not really. You're an annoying vulture at times, Manfred, but I never pegged you as a killer. I'm glad the sheriff released you."

It was his turn to be surprised. "That's very decent of you. I thought by now everyone would think I'd murdered Captain Lucky, even though the police had to exonerate me."

"What really happened to Captain Lucky?"

"Off the record?" He raised a brow.

"You're the newspaper man, not me. I know he was in some kind of trouble. That's why he needed the money I gave him. But why did he leave those pictures with you? He had to know how destructive they could be."

Manfred moved a step closer. "Captain Lucky was

in over his head. I think he really thought he could blackmail the seafolk for money, power, I don't know what. I can't imagine what possessed him. He thought if his pictures and video were safe with me, then he'd be safe too. What did he sell you?"

I couldn't see where it would hurt for him to know since it was now in police custody.

"He sold me a relic that he claimed could call the seafolk. I gave him five hundred dollars for it, which was nothing if he could have proved his claim. I imagine a celebrity newspaper would have given him a lot more with those pictures he gave you."

"But he didn't do that, even though my brief experience with Captain Lucky was that he took advantage of every situation. He was protecting himself, Mayor. He thought the person stalking him wouldn't kill him without the two things he gave us. I'm sure he was using them as lifelines to keep himself safe."

"So back to the seafolk killing him?"

He shrugged and adjusted his thick glasses. "He wasn't the only one in Duck involved with them, was he? There was you and Cathi Connor. But there was also Mr. Carl Lynch, the first mate on the Andalusia, waiting in the wings to take his place. I'm sure he's already moving his things into the Captain's stateroom, if they ever got it dried out."

"Was Cathi in one of the pictures with the merman? Is that how you know about her?"

"No. But she was afraid of it." His grin was nasty. "She begged me to give her the pictures. Let's face it, a school principle wouldn't last long if the public saw her cavorting with a merman, would she?"

It seemed like a good reason to kill Captain Lucky, although I already thought her plan to protect them at all costs was pretty good too. It was hard for me to believe Cathi would do anything like that. She was very proud of her reputation in the community.

But if she was sincere about leaving with Tovi and Lilly, her reputation wouldn't matter, would it?

That was all the time we had to talk. I wished I could have picked his brain a little more. He seemed to have more answers than I did. But the noise level in my small shop was enough to drive Treasure into hiding under some used clothes. I wanted to hide there with him.

I finally had to make the decision to close early for the day. I wasn't selling anything since the doorway was clogged with friends and neighbors. And Grandma Eleanore had begun looking tired and pale.

"Sorry, everyone, but you can imagine that my grandmother's health isn't good right now. We're going home, and I'd appreciate it if you'd give her some privacy."

While no one was happy about putting an end to the party, they left noisily, and I locked the front door behind them.

"Whew!" Grandma Eleanore used her hand to fan her face. "You'd think I was Doris Day or something. I guess everyone thinking you're dead and then you coming back makes you at least a small-time celebrity. I hope it won't always be this way."

"They'll get over it, especially now that the seafolk are here. There will be crazy sightings of them and lots of pictures that don't look like much of anything. That will take their minds off it—until the police figure out who killed Captain Lucky. That will be another circus."

"That's the way it's always been here," she confirmed. "I guess some things never change."

We went home in the golf cart. I half expected dozens of people to walk alongside or hang on to the cart. That didn't happen. A few people waved when they saw us, but that was more like normal. Even without the phenomenon of Grandma Eleanore, everyone in Duck waved to everyone else they knew all the time.

When we got back to the house, my grandmother started cooking up a storm. It looked like she was pulling everything down from the cabinets. We talked the whole time until Gramps got home, and then we ate the delicious meal she'd prepared while we talked some more.

"Gramps, have you looked at Carl Lynch, the first mate on the Andalusia, for Captain Lucky's death? I know Sheriff Riley had to let Manfred go. I guess he didn't have enough evidence to keep him. But what about the first mate? He gets Captain Lucky's job now. Maybe that's enough motive for murder."

He nodded. "I've talked to him, Dae. He and Mr. Vorst had great alibis for the time Captain Lucky was killed. And we just can't figure how that stateroom came to be like it was underwater. The thing is still soaked."

"Is this something new?" Grandma Eleanore asked. "We never discussed sheriff's business at the dinner table before."

Gramps smiled and touched her hand. "Sorry, sweetheart. You're right. It's not good for the digestion."

When she went into the pantry for something, Gramps leaned close to me. "Have you seen or talked to Mary Catherine? I haven't been able to get away but I know she's been hurt by this, Dae."

"I know. I haven't seen her since we left here this morning. I'll check on her."

When I went upstairs to check her bedroom, all her personal possessions were gone. The room was exactly as it had been before she'd moved in.

"She moved out," I told him a few minutes later. "I'll check on her later. Right now, I think I need to go see Kevin."

Grandma Eleanore was standing at the counter with two coffee cups in her hand. She made a loud sighing sound, called for Gramps, and then collapsed on the kitchen floor.

Chapter Twenty

"Call 911, Dae!" Gramps yelled.

I took out my phone, but before I could push the button, Grandma Eleanore sat up.

"I'm sorry. Don't call anyone, Dae. I'll be fine."

"We have to find out why this happened," Gramps told her. "You might need a doctor."

She patted his hand and smiled at him. "You always were a worry wart, Horace. There's nothing to worry about here. Dae, go see that young man of yours. Maybe he can come by for a while later."

"Okay." I glanced at Gramps.

"All right," he agreed. "But if it happens again, we go to the hospital, right?"

Grandma Eleanore nodded. "Good. Now help me

up. I don't want to lie around on the floor all day. I think I broke both those cups."

Gramps held her in his arms after we'd helped her up. "I don't care about the cups. Come and sit down. You've gone through a lot in the last twenty-four hours. You're probably exhausted."

"All right, Horace. Don't fuss. Let's sit down together for a while."

I was torn between leaving them and going to talk to Kevin. Gramps had everything under control, I finally realized. He was right. She was just tired after being chased around by all those people. It was best to let them have some time together.

I said goodbye and started down Duck Road, a little nervous despite the large crowd of people still on the streets. I really didn't want to see Tovi or Lilly that night. Things had become impossibly crazy. I needed a time to myself.

Grandma Eleanore would be fine. She was tired and had probably overdone it after the day she'd had. She just needed some down time, like I did. It wasn't good to be too excited by people harassing you about your personal life.

Even though I told myself that, I was still worried about her. I hoped the strain of coming back where she belonged wasn't too much. I kept thinking about what Kevin and Mary Catherine had said about her. They were wrong, of course. Everything was going to be just fine.

The moon was still waxing to full in the starry sky above me as I turned the corner to follow the road to the Blue Whale. It was darker here, away from the commercial lights around the Duck Shoppes. I stayed in the shadows, away from the other walkers and golf carts gliding up and down the road.

I was almost to the door at the inn when I saw Lilly. She was gazing at the stone mermaid in the fountain. There were five or six people on the verandah enjoying the cool night air. They didn't pay any attention to the young woman by the fountain. The shadows from the inn and the trees surrounding it hid her nakedness. Otherwise, I was sure there would have been a lot more commotion.

Lilly hadn't seen me yet. It was as though she was entranced by the mermaid in the fountain. I watched her until Cathi Connor came running up and led her away into the deeper shadows, leading back to the ocean behind the inn. Cathi seemed to be trying to explain to Lilly that she couldn't stand around naked in the moonlight, but I was only guessing at her words, too far away to actually hear them.

I was pretty sure Cathi was in love with the merman, but it seemed she'd taken on responsibility for his sister too. Maybe she was just trying to keep other photos of them, maybe better ones, from being taken.

Shrugging it off, I concentrated on what I was going to say to Kevin. I knew he'd be somewhere inside, probably getting the menu ready for the next day. I wasn't angry with him for pointing out the possible pitfalls of bringing Grandma Eleanore back to us—not really. I wanted to assure him that I'd heard his problems with the concept and that I had unknowingly brought her back. I hadn't set out to ignore him. It had just happened that way.

But when I reached the mostly darkened kitchen, I saw him with Tess, their discussion exchanged in low

tones over the wood table. I waited by the kitchen door
to find out what they were talking about.

"I think this is a brilliant plan to capture one of the
seafolk," Tess said. "We won't have to keep them for
long. Just a few minutes, and I'll have everything I
need."

Kevin was doodling on a piece of paper—I knew he
liked to write things down when he could. He loved
diagrams.

"We'll be very careful and respectful of whichever
one we catch," he said. "We have to make sure neither
of them is harmed in any way."

I couldn't stand to hear another moment of it. I
barged in on their conversation.

"You've got to be kidding. I asked you not to do
this, Kevin. It's wrong."

He sat back in his chair. "Sometimes we do things
even if other people think they're a mistake."

"Is that it?" I laughed. "I brought my grandmother
back against your better judgment, and now you're
going to trap one of the seafolk to get even with me?"

"Of course not, Dae." Tess got to her feet. "But if
we don't document the existence of this race, we may
never get another chance. We should understand them,
and if need be, protect them from our world."

"All of that just means more danger and crazy
people searching for them," I argued. "You should
know better, Kevin. You've worked with unusual
people before. Did it help to document them?"

He stood, too, and walked toward me. "Dae—"

"You can't make this right with a hug and a kiss," I
told him. "I'm going to warn Tovi and Lilly that you're
looking for them. Have a nice night."

Kevin walked after me, but I started running. When I glanced behind me, he was gone. I ran blindly through the night, crying, until I reached Duck Road.

I wouldn't let them experiment on the seafolk. It was always for their own good. Just like Grandma Eleanore's mother keeping her from her grandmother so she couldn't talk about her gift.

Some people just didn't understand.

Mary Catherine would. I went to the Pet Emporium where I saw a small light in the window behind the blinds. I knocked quickly at the door and waved to her when she peeked out at me.

"Dae! Come in. What's wrong?"

Looking around at the changes she'd made to the shop, I knew she planned to live here for a while. It was against the rental company's rules, but everyone did it, at least occasionally. I'd done it more than once.

"You didn't have to leave the house," I told her. "No one wanted you to go."

Her sharp green eyes looked away from me. "It was a little awkward since I'd planned to leave a lot sooner, but Horace had asked me to stay. We're both grownups, Dae. I was beginning to think of your grandfather as more than just a friend, you know. I don't think that's possible now."

I sighed and sat in one of the green velvet chairs she used for consultations. "I'm sorry. I know you're right. I didn't mean to make your life more complicated."

She sat opposite me on the edge of her makeshift bed. "Don't worry about me. I always move on. After being a widow five times, I know that's what you have to do."

"But you can't live at the shop forever. Are you still going to stay in Duck?"

"I think so. As soon as the crowds clear out, I'll probably go stay with Kevin. I love the Blue Whale Inn. I don't think he'd mind a permanent guest, do you?"

"I might not be the best person to ask what Kevin minds. He and I have had a falling out."

"Oh, no. You two are so good together. What's the problem?"

I picked up a dog collar from a side table. It was new so the only impression I had of it was when it was made in a Chinese factory and transported here.

"It's the mermaid issue." I shook my head. "And the issue with my grandmother. Kevin thinks I brought her back despite his feelings on the subject. I think he wants to spite me now by helping Tess catch a mermaid."

"That's a mistake," she agreed. "Whether he thinks bringing your grandmother back was a bad idea or not, catching the mermaid isn't good. But I can't believe Kevin would be that petty either."

"It's not just that," I admitted. "Once I convinced him that there were seafolk, I think he really believes he'll be helping by documenting them. I think Tess's heart is in the right place too, but I'm just worried what will happen if they accomplish it."

"I don't blame you." She ran her hand through her hair. "Maybe I should try talking to Kevin too. I'm not emotionally involved like you are. He might listen."

"Whatever you can do. He and I are butting heads right now. I don't know what else I can say to him. I saw Lilly by the Blue Whale tonight. Cathi Connor got her off the street. The seafolk need a stash of clothes for when they come to visit. They'd stand out a lot less if they weren't naked."

She laughed, and so did I. We had some plum wine together, and then I went home. There was still no sign of Tovi or Lilly. I hoped Cathi would keep them inside until dawn. Maybe Tess and Kevin could still be reasoned with before anyone made a mistake.

Gramps and Grandma Eleanore had gone up to their room when I got back. I snuggled with Treasure in my bed and thought about all the changes that would take place now that she was back.

I knew Gramps would be happier and it would be easier to move to the Blue Whale—if Kevin and I actually got married. Knowing Gramps wasn't alone was a big thing for me.

But if questions about my grandmother became more in depth, Gramps and I needed to come up with a good story as to where she had been and how she'd come back. Not that anyone would guess that I'd brought her back from where she was trapped in time, but it was a good idea to sort through the details. I had a feeling that Manfred Vorst wouldn't be satisfied with the answers we'd given so far.

Treasure and I finally fell asleep. I was dreaming about my mother—not my usual dreams of her sitting in her car underwater—a dream of her as a teenager at the fair. Probably the carnival that Grandma Eleanore had described.

She was sitting in a dark tent with weird lighting. There was a man opposite her. He was young, good-looking in a dark, possibly malevolent way. His eyes were like black diamonds in his swarthy face. His black hair was long and shaggy around his shoulders. He wore a nicely cut black suit that looked expensive.

And he was holding my mother's hand.

She was very young. Her hair was different, longer than she'd ever worn it after I was born. She looked like she might be in high school with the promise of the future in her glowing face and bright eyes.

"What do you see in my future?" she asked the dark man in a high-pitched, childish voice.

He stroked the palm of her hand in a sensual manner and then looked around the candlelit room with a narrowed gaze.

"I see someone who doesn't belong here, Jean. Does the name 'Dae' seem like something you might name your child?"

Chapter Twenty-one

I woke before she could answer. My heart was racing, and my mouth was dry. Treasure protested as I set him aside to get a drink of water.

Had that man really seen me?

Was that the psychic Grandma Eleanore said I could use to communicate with my mother?

If so, he certainly was menacing and scary. He obviously was a real psychic from his words to my mother and the impression he'd given my grandmother. But it would be hard to trust him.

Granted I'd only known a few other psychics in my life—Kevin's former FBI partner and fiancé, Mary Catherine and her ability to communicate with animals, and my friend, Shayla, who'd tried so hard to bring my mother back to speak with me were among them.

The man with my mother was much more frightening and more difficult to understand. I could feel his force directed toward me in that room. Of course he was in the past and couldn't really hurt me.

Still, the dream had left me rattled. I needed to talk with my grandmother again about her feelings toward him. Something had caused her to recommend that I use him to speak to my mother.

Still feeling unbalanced, I went up on the widow's walk and leaned against the iron rail as I looked at the town below me. Traffic had died down to just a few cars and pedestrians on Duck Road. Everything looked quiet and serene with the bright moon hanging above us.

Tomorrow, our Fourth of July crowd would begin going home. Some would stay, and others would arrive until the summer season was past. Nothing was ever as large and difficult—or as rewarding—for the full-time citizens of Duck. It was the way the world had always been here, feast or famine. Our ancestors had survived, and we would too.

I sighed and went back down the stairs, wondering if what Manfred had suggested was true. If the seafolk hadn't killed Captain Lucky because he'd threatened to expose them, had Cathi done it to keep her name and face out of the newspaper? Or could it have been Carl Lynch to get the lavish stateroom and captain's title?

Lying back on the bed with Treasure, I was almost asleep again when my cell phone rang.

It was Mary Catherine. Her voice was a whisper on the phone.

"Come to the Blue Whale quickly, Dae," she said. "Tess and Kevin have trapped Lilly. We have to set her free."

Anger and fear rushed through me as I agreed to get there as fast as I could. I pulled on shorts, a top, and sandals. Treasure whined as he followed me downstairs. I shushed him and kept moving, murmuring an explanation of why he couldn't go with me.

I was surprised when Gramps didn't wake up. Maybe that was why he'd begun sleeping in the recliner after my mother had died. He was afraid he wouldn't catch me sneaking out of the house. The idea made me smile as I stepped out into the moonlit night.

The electric golf cart was quiet. It was slow too, but still faster than I could run to the inn. I hated that Mary Catherine was out there alone. And I was furious that Kevin and Tess had trapped Lilly. I hoped they had been very careful when they'd set their trap and that she was unharmed.

I was passing the line of trees that separated my house from the Duck Shoppes when Tovi sprang into the cart. One minute, the seat beside me was empty, and the next he was there.

"How did you learn to jump that way?" I demanded after my heart stopped pounding at the surprise.

"I don't know. It has always been this way. Perhaps you should ask the lady scientist who has trapped my sister in a net." He sounded as though his teeth were on edge as he spoke.

"It was stupid to trap her," I told him as a part of an apology. "My friend and I will release her."

"I was on my way to do the same. I will never understand humans. We see you diving in the ocean, exploring your wrecked ships. We don't attempt to trap you or keep you under the water with us."

"Don't make it sound like you're that different," I said. "You used to be human. You understand some of how we are. We just want to understand you. People don't believe in mermaids and mermen."

"Our only defense," he snickered. "It must stay this way, or seafolk are doomed. You know this. Why defend what these people have done?"

"Because I know both of them and I know they mean well. They're a little excited and carried away with trying to make sure everyone respects your people."

"Bah. I remember being human well enough to know that you can't stand not to explore and destroy. You even destroy each other. There is no logic or understanding."

My foot was down so hard on the golf cart accelerator that it rattled along on the street like an amusement park ride. Gramps wouldn't like to know that I was driving his baby so roughly, but there was no time to waste.

"Did you kill Captain Lucky from the gambling ship to keep your picture secret? Did you do it to protect Cathi?"

"I had no reason to kill him. He meant nothing to me. I could swim away and not return for years until I was forgotten."

"But you just said secrecy is the only thing keeping your people alive."

"I don't have to explain myself to you." Tovi

grinned at me before he jumped out of the golf cart as we approached the inn. I saw his shadow running along the edge of the road and then he disappeared.

I took a deep breath and pulled around the side of the building. The golf cart was hidden from sight by the side of the inn's high blue wall and a few trees.

What was I going to do? Tess and Kevin weren't my enemies. They didn't even realize what they were doing. All I had to do was find Lilly and free her. Once that was done, I could go home. But how difficult was that going to be?

"Dae!"

It was Mary Catherine—I almost jumped out of my skin.

"You shouldn't sneak up on people that way."

"Sorry. I just wanted you to know that I was here." She adjusted her pink sweatpants. "It's much easier communicating with other animals. Humans are so excitable."

"It's okay," I murmured. "I just had a surprise visit from Tovi."

"You mean he's out here too?"

"I'm afraid so. He knows about Lilly and wants to free her. How did you find out?"

"Kevin and Tess awakened a pelican. As soon as he realized what was going on, he got back with me." She put a hand to her head. "They have painful mental patterns."

"Okay. Where's Lilly?"

"They snagged her at the end of the pier. I don't know why they went off and left her there, but this is our chance to free her."

"Ladies." Manfred Vorst's voice was distinctive in

the darkness. "I assume we're all out here for the same reason."

Mary Catherine groaned. "Go away. There's nothing to report here. Leave us alone."

"I disagree. A little bird told me that someone captured a mermaid out here. You haven't seen anything like that, have you?"

"A little bird?" Mary Catherine sounded angry. "Those darn pelicans don't know when to keep their big mouths shut."

"What?" Manfred asked.

"Never mind. She's right. There's nothing going on out here."

"Then why are you out here, Mayor?"

We heard a screech come from the darkness near the water and started running in that direction. There was still plenty of time to get Lilly out of the trap before sunrise. We had to work fast though, and despite Manfred, if we could.

It wasn't like Kevin to start a plan and not finish it. I was surprised that he and Tess hadn't waited with Lilly, doing whatever Tess had decided needed to be done. It was another way I could tell Kevin's heart wasn't in it.

"Where are we going?" Manfred asked. "We're going to fall in the water. I can't see a thing."

"Maybe you should go home then," I suggested. "It can be dangerous out here. I'd hate to see you get hurt."

"No, thanks." He chuckled, beginning to sound out of breath. "I go where you go."

Mary Catherine stopped first. She sat down on one of the pretty benches that I'd helped Kevin pick out for the back garden that led to the shore.

"Go ahead," she said breathlessly. "I have to rest for a minute. You get her, Dae."

"Okay." I kept running.

"I assume your friend, Kevin Brickman, caught the mermaid," Manfred huffed. "I guess he was in need of a little company since you've given him the cold shoulder lately."

"Shut up. Go away."

By that time, he couldn't answer, just making a few groaning noises.

As I reached the end of the pier, a set of bright spotlights came on. Kevin had installed at the back of the Blue Whale for night time events. I was blinded for a moment, took a misstep, and ended up with my feet in the surf.

Manfred fell face-first in the water. I would've laughed, but I didn't have the breath for it.

Tovi ran out on the pier, and I jumped back up on it to follow him.

"What's going on out here?" Kevin called from the inn. "Is that you, Mary Catherine?"

Mary Catherine replied, but I wasn't sure what she said. I didn't stop to find out. Lights had also come on along the edge of the pier. I could see the large, heavy net and Tovi going after it with his bare hands.

Of course I hadn't thought to bring a big knife or even scissors to cut the net. How was I going to get Lilly out? Tovi was strong and agile, but that wouldn't help with a heavy-gauge, modern net.

"Dae?" Kevin followed us out on the pier. "What's going on? Why are all of you out here?"

"Don't pretend you didn't catch the mermaid," I

said. "We're here to let her go. I can't believe you did this."

"I'm not here to let her go," Manfred said. "I want all the pictures I can get. And interviews, if you're up for them. If not, I'll just make up my own caption."

"This is crazy," Kevin protested. "I didn't catch anyone. Tess and I decided against the plan. We didn't want the world to get any crazier than it is already."

"You didn't?" I smiled at him, thinking how much I loved him.

"No. You were right. Tess and I had some brandy last night, and she went home."

"Help me," Tovi yelled. "I can't break the net, and it has begun moving away from the pier."

"What?" Kevin asked.

"It's attached to a boat," I guessed. "We have to break her free."

It was too dark to see the boat that was offshore, tugging the net behind it. Lilly screamed and struggled against it, but she couldn't get out.

"I'll get a knife," Kevin yelled as he headed back toward the inn.

"There's no time." I jumped from the end of the pier and grabbed the net.

"Dae!" Mary Catherine shouted. "What in the world are you doing?"

I couldn't answer as the net began to sink into the warm, salty water. I saw Lilly's terrified face before I went under. Tovi was beside me, gnawing at the rope with his teeth. I knew that wouldn't work.

The boat was pulling all three of us away from the shore toward an unknown destination. It was easy to imagine that someone had realized the value of having a mermaid. This was what Tovi had expected.

It was bad for Tovi and Lilly, but it was worse for me since the net quickly sank completely. At least they could breathe under water.

Chapter Twenty-two

I felt Tovi cover me, his chest against my back. He lifted my chin and breathed air into my mouth. Lilly, still on the inside of the net, clung in front of me. Between the two of them, I was able to breathe.

The movement of the net had picked up speed. The cable dragging it wasn't long enough to allow it to sink to the bottom. We followed along behind the boat about ten feet from the surface.

Despite the assistance from the two seafolk, I was still terrified. What if the boat captain changed his mind and cut the net free? Or perhaps worse, what would be waiting for us if they pulled us up and dropped us on deck like a haul of tuna?

The current and temperature changed as we got out in deeper water. How far did the boat plan to go? It wasn't like the gambling ship where they had to reach international waters to run their games. The government wasn't interested in Tovi and Lilly. What were they waiting for?

It seemed as though my answers were coming as the pull from the boat slowed and the net sank another few feet. The cable immediately began to haul the net and its cargo to the deck. We were suddenly free of the water and held suspended about twenty feet above the boat and her crew.

I rubbed my eyes and took a deep, grateful breath of the night air. The men below us were talking and staring at us. Did they think I was a mermaid too? Should I shout to them to release us so they'd know I wasn't?

"Are you all right, Dae?" Tovi asked.

"I'm fine, but I'll never go fishing again."

"What are they waiting for?" Lilly asked. "If they're going to hack us to pieces, why don't they lower us to the deck and get it over with?"

"Let's not encourage any hasty action," I said. "Maybe they just want to look at you."

Then I heard the high-pitched squeal of a microphone. Someone hit a piece of wood with a gavel.

"What do I hear for the first bid on the female aquatic creature?" A man's voice began auctioning Lilly. Dozens of rapid bids followed the first.

"Animals," Tovi snarled. "We need something sharp to get out of this. We can dive into the water from here."

"I think there's only one thing to do. I'll create a

distraction. Be ready for your chance to get away."

"What are you going to do, Dae?" Lilly asked.

"Just be ready," I told her. "And don't worry about me or look back. The two of you just get in the water."

Tovi started to voice another protest, but I cut him off.

"Hey! Hey, you people down there. What's going on? Let me out of here. I'm not a mermaid. I'm Dae O'Donnell, Mayor of Duck, North Carolina. I suggest you let me go before the Coast Guard gets here."

The auction stopped, and the crowd of men on deck began talking loudly and pointing at the net. I didn't recognize any of them, but I knew the man who came to see why the auction had stopped.

Dillon Guthrie.

From his recent emails, I had no idea that he was close to Duck. I thought he was still diving for lost artifacts in South America. I knew he was capable of anything from smuggling to murder if it made a profit. Selling a few seafolk, probably to collectors, was possible for him.

"Dae?" he yelled back at me. "Is that really you? I should have known you'd be in the thick of things."

"Dillon. What are you doing here?"

"What I always do—follow the treasure. I heard about this particular treasure and had to see it for myself. You know how I am." He chuckled. "I go where the money is."

I heard him give the order for the net to be slowly lowered to the deck. One of his crew followed through, and the thick netting began to sink.

My eyes scanned the deck. The yacht was huge and extravagantly-appointed. Not as big as the Andalusia

II, but a very nice size. Only the best for Dillon.

I was searching for anything I could grab and throw back to Tovi and Lilly that they could use to cut the net. On my first pass, I didn't see anything, but my eyes were burning from the sea water, and my vision wasn't as good as it could be.

All the people on deck moved out of the way for the net, creating a circle around where we came down. Several crewmembers stood at attention with rifles in their hands, their eyes glued on their captives.

"Captain." Dillon nodded to the short, round man who immediately jumped to do his bidding.

"Let me help you out there, Miss." The stubby captain offered his hand to me.

Tovi was still outside the net, as I was. He had the best chance to get away.

Dillon must have realized the same thing. He pointed to one of the crewmembers, and that man fired a dart into Tovi's back. The merman dropped to the deck. Lilly screamed and reached for him.

Once I was untangled from the net, I wasted no time marching up to Dillon and demanding that he release them.

"You know this is wrong. They could be the last two of their kind for all you know. Let them go, Dillon. You have plenty of money. Be compassionate for once."

He reached a hand to my bedraggled clothes. "Steward, escort Mayor O'Donnell below deck to change. I'm sure you'll find something in your size there, Dae. Come back up, and we'll talk."

In the meantime, he'd be auctioning his cargo.

I swept a frantic search across the deck again but didn't see anything that could cut the net and release

Lilly. I figured she could grab Tovi and jump overboard if she was free, but there was nothing to accommodate my plans.

"All right. Fine. Don't do anything until I get back." I knew he'd ignore me. But I stood a better chance below deck of finding something useful.

"No!" Lilly called out. "Don't leave us, Dae."

Her call made my stomach twist in knots, but I ignored her and followed the steward below deck. I couldn't explain what I had in mind.

The man led me to a small stateroom that was tastefully decorated with sea motifs. There were also clothes of different sizes in the closet, most still with store tags on them, and a variety of toiletries in the bathroom. I pulled on a striped sundress, shorter than I liked, but it was quick. I'd lost my sandals in the ocean and found a pair my size.

The whole time, my mind was trying to formulate a plan to save my friends. I found scissors and a small paring knife in the suite, but neither of those tools would cut through the net. I ran a brush through my hair and went to the door, scanning the passageway for crewmembers.

No one was there. I started wondering where I could find something I could use. The galley? I ran down the passageway until I found it. But none of the knives looked sharp enough to cut through an industrial net. Maybe Dillon was paranoid about his chef having deadly utensils.

I left the galley, headed toward the engine room, and passed a closet marked utility. The door wasn't locked, and I found a large pair of cutters inside. My sundress wasn't big enough to conceal much of anything. I ran back to the stateroom and grabbed a shawl I'd seen in the closet.

Lilly wasn't going to have much time to cut the net and escape, I realized. Even though they wouldn't shoot them, they obviously didn't mind tranquilizing them. My brain felt as though it was moving a hundred miles an hour as it went through all the places the cutters had been before they'd reached the utility room. Thank goodness the clothes and shawl were new. There wasn't much involved in my awareness of them.

I saw the stairs going up to the deck and pasted my big mayor's smile on my face as I ascended them. I was wearing the pink shawl, but had the clippers wrapped in the ends of it. If I could get close enough to the net, I could free Lilly before anyone even noticed.

The auction appeared to be over—I was right about that part. Tovi was still lying on the deck. Lilly was crying softly, her head bent over her legs that would become a tail as soon as she hit the water. The winners and losers were enjoying caviar and champagne as they ogled the two captives.

"There you are." Dillon slipped an arm around me. His hand missed the end of the clippers by less than an inch. "You look great, Dae." He kissed my cheek. "How is your little shop doing?"

"Missing Pieces is fine. Are you back for the third Augustine bell?"

It was the only attraction and mutual love that we shared—antiques and ancient societies.

"I knew you were a good bet to find the third bell." He sipped his champagne from a crystal flute. "It's your gift, attracting missing objects to you. I wish you'd come to Jamestown with me. It was incredible. I can't wait to show you my finds."

I almost didn't recognize him. It was his voice that made me realize it was Dillon. He'd changed during his last treasure hunt, doing most of the diving himself. He was tan and fit with streaks of sun blond in his dark hair. He and I were almost the same height, but his shoulders and chest were muscular.

He'd asked me to go on the treasure hunt to the sunken pirate city of Jamestown, but I'd turned him down. I wanted to see those strange and amazing things that he'd offered to show me, but I was tied to Duck with my heart.

"I can't wait to see the pictures." I reasoned that there was no point in alienating him and giving away my plot to free Lilly and Tovi. I accepted a glass of champagne and smiled.

"So what's this about your seafolk?" He grinned. "Worried that you won't get your share of the treasure?"

"No, Dillon. I know you'll do anything for money, but this is like selling slaves. You have to let them go."

"You know I'd do almost anything for you, Dae. But this is business. I've already auctioned your little seafolk. Will your conscience keep you from taking part of the profits?"

"I can't." I turned away from him. "I won't do this. No amount of money would convince me. You know me that well."

One of the men in a sharkskin suit called Dillon and beckoned to him. He left me standing there, only a few feet from Lilly. She stared up at me, her strange eyes questioning what I would do next.

A crewmember made the space between me and

the net even shorter as he walked by with crackers and caviar. I reached for it and managed to upset his tray. Everything fell on the deck, and two other crew members came to his aid.

I managed to do a quick step around them as they tried to clean up. The net was against my leg, so I barely had to reach to cut a large part of it.

"Get Tovi and get away," I whispered.

"Thank you." Lilly got on her feet and put one hand through the hole.

I hid her movements as she extricated herself from the net. Tovi was only a yard away from us. He was starting to awaken, shaking his head and looking around.

"He's awake, sir," A crewmember with a rifle told Dillon. "You want me to lay him out again?"

Dillon responded with a laugh. "He doesn't belong to me anymore. Ask Mr. Smith what he wants to do."

All eyes turned to the man in the sharkskin suit. He was smearing caviar on a cracker and carefully balancing his champagne flute in the other hand.

There wouldn't be a better opportunity.

"Go now," I said to Lilly.

"But what about you?" she asked.

"He won't do anything to hurt me. Go now!"

Lilly didn't wait for another invitation. She grabbed Tovi in her arms and threw herself over the side. A huge splash came up and shot water crystals into the boat.

All the crewmembers ran to the side of the yacht, but it was too late. Tovi and Lilly had disappeared into the gray Atlantic. They would never find them.

Chapter Twenty-three

"Do you know how much that little stunt just cost me, Dae?" Dillon thundered.

"It was wrong. They weren't things or treasures that could be found and sold. You had to let them go."

I had no doubt I could convince Dillon of the rightness of Lilly and Tovi being free. I wasn't worried about what he would do to me. He cared about me in some weird way. I knew he wouldn't hurt me.

"Try telling that to the people who bought them and now can't take them home."

"Just give them their money back," I suggested. "I'm sure they won't care."

"Honey, you don't know the kind of people I do business with." He reached out and ran his hand through my hair. "They want your head since they can't have a mermaid."

There wasn't much I could say to that. I was pretty sure that wouldn't happen. On the other hand, I knew he ran with a wealthy, dangerous crowd. Dillon was well-known for delivering the goods—drugs, treasures—if he said he had it, he had it. It was his reputation.

A discreet knock at the stateroom door where Dillon had taken me brought the steward in.

"Mr. Guthrie, your guests are leaving. They request your presence."

I heard the whir of a helicopter as he spoke.

"All right, Jones. I'll be right up." When the steward was gone, Dillon smiled at me. "You owe me, Dae. You say you have the third Augustine bell?"

"I said a man came into the shop who said he had the bell. I can find him."

"You do that. I'll be in touch."

He left me in the stateroom with specific instructions not to leave. No problem. Those caviar-eating customers on deck weren't exactly my type. I didn't have any reason to make friends with them, and if staying here spared my life, I'd stay.

But then I heard the sound of another vessel approaching. Apparently many of Dillon's customers onboard had their own transportation within a short call away. I thought this was just another one of those until I heard a man's voice on a loud speaker.

"Ahoy, Jamestown," the voice said. "This is the Coast Guard. We are searching for Mayor Dae O'Donnell on a rescue mission. Please advise if you have seen her."

It was getting light. I looked out the porthole and saw the gleaming blue and white Coast Guard vessel in close proximity. Gramps and Kevin were on the bow with the captain in his uniform.

"Looks like my ride is here." I ran out of the stateroom and headed to the deck, despite Dillon's orders.

The helicopter I'd heard had pontoons and was floating in the water beside Dillon's vessel. Two other luxury yachts were close by, their passengers being picked up by skiffs heading from them to the Jamestown.

"Dae, I told you to stay below," Dillon protested.

I waved to Gramps and Kevin with both hands. "I'm going home. It looks like most of your party is over. I guess I'll see you later."

He grabbed my hand. "I would never hurt you. You know that, right? I would've taken you back to Duck after everyone left."

"I know." I smiled at him. "At least I was pretty sure. Thanks for telling me."

"You know we could be awesome together." He grinned and took my other hand, turning me away from the Coast Guard ship. "There's no treasure we couldn't find. Your Missing Pieces could be a world market."

What could I say? Dillon had always represented a siren's song for me. Yes, he was bad. He'd done terrible things. But he and I both had our hearts wrapped up in the mysteries of the past. I could never be with him the way he wanted. Our only attraction was this one shared love.

"I think you remind me too much of my pirate

ancestor, Rafe Masterson. I don't want to live your life. You don't belong in mine. Come to Missing Pieces when you can, and we'll settle up the bells. But that's all we have together, Dillon. I'm sorry."

He smiled sadly and leaned his head closer to kiss my cheek. "I like that you think of me as a pirate, Dae, since I know how much you like them. I'll drop by soon. In the meantime, what are you going to tell the Coast Guard?"

"The truth. I fell off the pier looking for the mermaid and got tangled in your fishing net."

"Good story. I think you have more pirate blood in you than you think."

Dillon sent me to the Coast Guard ship in a skiff. A member of the crew helped me out of the boat and up the ladder to the deck.

Gramps and Kevin were quick to hug me and welcome me aboard. The Coast Guard captain insisted on debriefing me before he would allow Dillon's yacht to leave.

I told him exactly what I'd told Dillon I would say. The captain was skeptical at first, since someone had mentioned that I'd been kidnapped.

"Are you sure no one coerced you into being aboard the *Jamestown*?" he demanded.

"Absolutely not. I was there by my own choice after Mr. Guthrie brought me up from his fishing net."

"All right, Mayor O'Donnell," he said. "Thank you for your statement. I'm glad you're safe. We'll head back now. Maybe next time, you should hunt for mermaids during the day."

My decision not to press charges against Dillon wasn't popular with Gramps or Kevin.

"The man is a criminal, Dae," Gramps reminded me.

"I'm not denying that or that what he did with Lilly and Tovi was wrong. But he didn't kidnap me. That was my choice to hold on to the net. I was lucky to survive."

"How did you make it that far out in a fishing net?" Kevin asked.

"Tovi and Lilly shared their breath with me."

Kevin's blue/gray eyes were even more unhappy with that idea.

"I'm glad you're okay, honey," Gramps said. "But you should've helped the Coast Guard take Guthrie into custody and impound his yacht."

There was no point in arguing with him. We were never going to see eye-to-eye on Dillon. I wasn't even sure I understood how I felt about him. How could I explain it to Kevin or Gramps?

The return trip to Duck was much more comfortable than it had been leaving. We pulled in close to where the Andalusia was berthed. I'd forgotten there was going to be a large re-launch to celebrate the ship opening for business again.

I was a mess and cringed at the idea of representing the town at the event. Lucky for me that Cody, Rick Treyburn, and Dab Efird were there. There were also TV news crews, and Manfred Vorst on hand taking pictures.

Me, Gramps, and Kevin sneaked off the Coast Guard ship and made it past the crowd of spectators who were there to get free passes to the slot machines for the day. Several of the Duck businesses were also there to give out free donuts, surf board rentals, and video game passes.

But despite all that, Manfred's eagle eye landed on me before I could leave the pier.

"Mayor O'Donnell!" He shouted above the music and Captain Carl Lynch's speech. He ran over to us as he flipped a page on his notebook. "Welcome back. I heard you were rescued by an old friend. What was Dillon Guthrie doing sailing in these waters?"

"No comment." Gramps grabbed my arm and pushed past him. "She's been through enough today. Give her some space."

Manfred moved, only because Gramps and Kevin both got in front of me. "Okay. Later, then, huh? At your office or Missing Pieces? You know I'm always around."

I didn't say anything. He was right. At some point I'd have to answer his questions just to keep him from following me around. I knew my story, and I was sticking to it. I wouldn't include Lilly and Tovi. They'd been in the news enough.

There were dozens of golf carts waiting by the ticket office at the end of the pier, but Gramps's or Kevin's weren't among them. Gramps held open the back door to his police car, and I got in. Kevin got in beside me, and Gramps maneuvered the car out of the parking lot.

"I'm sorry I thought you and Tess had set a trap for Lilly and Tovi," I said to Kevin. "I should've known you'd realize it was the wrong thing to do."

"I guess we don't know each other as well as we thought," he responded.

He still sounded angry. I realized we hadn't had the opportunity to talk and smooth everything over about Grandma Eleanore and the seafolk, much less about Dillon. I wasn't worried. We'd figure out a way.

"The crime lab can't even find DNA on that hunk of coral you gave me," Gramps explained. "I'm afraid we're at a dead end for Captain Lucky's murder. Unless we want to catch your seafolk and charge them."

"I don't think they're to blame. May I have the horn back? How is Grandma Eleanore doing?"

"She seems to be fine," Gramps replied. "While you were out chasing mermaids, we were coming up with a plausible story for everyone. The repercussions of her sudden appearance may go on longer than the usual gossip in Duck. A few people—Mad Dog and August Grandin—are calling for my resignation until her reappearance can be explained."

"What do they think happened?" I asked. "Do they think you were hiding her in the attic all these years?"

"I don't know." Gramps eased the police car into the parking lot at town hall. "I'll be glad when Ronnie is back and can take over all this mess. I'd forgotten what a pain it is."

"When is he supposed to come back?" Kevin asked.

"I don't know right now. Probably six weeks or so. I think Eleanore and I are going for a long trip somewhere as soon as he takes over again. We always wanted to go to Hawaii. Didn't have the time for it back then. I have plenty of time for it now."

Gramps looked pleased with himself. He smiled as he opened the back door for me. "Let's go inside, and I'll get that coral for you. If you don't want to sell it, Dae, maybe you can keep it on your desk."

"I've heard a lot of talk about Duck being named

the mermaid capital of the world," Kevin said with a
wry grin. "I like that better than all the other
distinctions they give towns."

"Me too." I rolled the idea around in my head.
"Maybe we could make Duck a safe haven for
mermaids. Like they do with birds and butterflies."

"At least birds and butterflies exist," Gramps
reminded me. "I still haven't seen one of these
creatures."

"I have," Kevin volunteered. "More than once. It's
so amazing that I can hardly believe it—like looking up
one day and seeing a dragon flying across the sky."

Gramps chuckled as we walked into town hall.
"You've been spending too much time with my
granddaughter, Brickman. You're losing your edge.
What kind of lawman does that?"

"The retired, innkeeper kind, sir. I don't mind
losing that edge at all."

I grabbed the coral horn from police lockup—I had
to sign for it—and Kevin walked home with me. I
planned to be at Missing Pieces all day but needed to
change clothes. It made me smile when I saw him
checking out my really short skirt. I didn't say
anything. It was good for a fiancé to still think you
were attractive.

We didn't talk much. Traffic on Duck Road was
heavy and made conversation difficult, but when we
reached the house, he put his hand on mine to stop me
from going inside.

"I'm sorry that we had this disagreement about
your grandmother and the seafolk," he said. "I didn't
mean to be an ass about either one. I was just worried
about you."

"I know." I touched his face and kissed him. "This thing with Grandma Eleanore isn't something I plan on doing again. Good thing, since I'm not really sure what I did. I just felt like it was wrong to leave her there. Now that she's back, we can be a family."

"Sure. I hope it works out for you. You know that."

"But you're still skeptical."

"Yes. That's okay. I can be wrong. Who knew there were seafolk walking around Duck?"

I hugged him, and we laughed. Everything seemed fine. Life was very sweet knowing Gramps would be happy, and I'd have someone to talk to about all the aspects of my gift.

"I have to get back to the Blue Whale to get ready for the hungry crowds at lunch."

"It shouldn't be so bad now. A lot of people are going home after the holiday."

"Except for the thousands coming in to look for mermaids," he reminded me.

"Except for those. I wish I had more mermaid merchandise at Missing Pieces. I think that's going to be a hot commodity for a while."

We parted happily. I watched him walk down the drive and around the bushes that kept our house mostly hidden from Duck Road. I was glad things were better between us. It would be nice if we never argued again, but I knew better. What was important was making up afterward.

I let myself in the house. It seemed very quiet.

"Grandma? Grandma Eleanore?" I knew she was here because Gramps had asked her to stay inside until their stories were set up. "Grandma?"

"Dae." Her weak voice filtered down the stairs to

me.

"Hold on. I'm coming."

I ran upstairs to find her on the bedroom floor. I'd never seen another person—not even a dead one—so pale. There was no color in her skin at all. Even the light brown highlights left in her graying hair were gone.

"What happened? Did you fall? Are you hurt? Let me help you get on the bed."

Nothing seemed to be broken as I helped her to her feet, but she was so weak that she had to lean against me to stand. We got to the bed, and she sagged across the quilt that she'd made before I was born.

"Let me call Gramps and an ambulance." I took out my cell phone. "I guess we should've done that yesterday when you fell. I'm sorry."

She took my hand and smiled. "Yes, please call your grandfather. Forget the ambulance. It won't do any good. This was going to happen, sweetheart. I couldn't stay here forever."

Chapter Twenty-four

I quickly called Gramps and told him to come home right away. He didn't ask any questions—just got off the phone. I knew he'd be squealing into the drive again.

"You'll be fine," I assured her. "But I think we should call an ambulance. You probably just need to have some tests done. Once they find out what's wrong with you, it'll be okay."

"It won't be." Her breath rattled in her chest. "I knew as soon as you brought me back that it wouldn't take long for it to catch up with me. You can't fool time, Dae. You have to work with it and respect it."

"No. Don't say that. You're not that old. You're

probably suffering from something like jetlag. I've noticed how tired I get when I use my gift to go back even for a few minutes. You just need some rest."

I dragged the quilt up over her as I heard Gramps's car in the drive.

"Gramps is here. I'm sure he'll want to call someone, at least a doctor." Tears gathered in my eyes. I knew what she was trying to say—the same thing Kevin and Mary Catherine had tried to tell me.

"Don't cry," she urged in a wispy voice. "You gave me a wonderful gift. Getting to know you and see what you grew up to be has been like a dream. I even had a chance to say goodbye to your grandfather. I didn't have that before. You gave that to me, Dae. And I love you for it."

I could hear Gramps's boots clunking up the stairs at a faster than normal rate. He kept calling our names, but I couldn't answer though the thick tears in my throat.

"What's going on?" He finally reached us, out of breath. "Did she fall again? Why didn't you call an ambulance, Dae? You know it takes them forever to get here. Maybe we can get her downstairs and take her to the hospital in the car."

"There's no reason to take me anywhere, Horace." She took his hand with her free one. "I'm just glad you made it back in time. This is the goodbye we never had."

"What are you saying?" His knees gave way as he knelt next to the bed. "You just got back. You'll be fine, Eleanore. You can't leave me again so soon."

"I love you, Horace." She smiled at both of us. Her hands were so weak she could barely squeeze ours. "I love you too, Dae. The two of you take good care of each other. Horace, you could smile a little more often. Dae, you take care using your gift. Don't make the same mistake I did and lose so much of your life."

She exhaled and let go of our hands. Her eyes closed, and she was gone. An immediate change began to come over her. She was crumbling away like dust. It only took a moment, and her body wasn't there.

"What in the world?" Gramps asked in a low voice as tears ran down his face. "What happened? Why did she die? And is she dead this time or just stuck out there again?"

"She's gone this time." A sob caught in my throat. I could barely speak. "When we go back in time, we can't stay. She couldn't stay here for the same reason. At least she's free now."

His voice was brusque as he got to his feet. "Free? She's just gone, Dae. Disintegrated. T-there's nothing left of her."

"Time caught up with her. She didn't belong here."

"So you knew this was going to happen?"

"No. I didn't." I stared at him through my tears. "But she was happy to be here even for a short while. She was glad she got to say goodbye."

"That's just not enough." He stormed out of the room. "And now what am I going to tell people about her being back and gone again? I don't know if I can handle this."

He was yelling all the way down the stairs. The front door slammed, and the engine started in the police car.

After a few minutes, I gathered the bed sheets and walked to the back of our property that ended at the

Currituck Sound. The day was sunny, but the winds swept across Duck with summer fierceness.

I sighed as I shook the sheets and watched what was left of Grandma Eleanore disappear into the wind and water. I sank down on the rocks and didn't move for hours. It was dark before Kevin's voice called from the backyard.

"Out here," I yelled back, grabbing the sheets and heading toward the house.

He hugged me. "I just heard from Horace what happened. I'm so sorry, Dae. Is there anything I can do?"

"No. She's gone." I looked up at him. "You and Mary Catherine were right. I shouldn't have interfered."

"That's not true. Horace told me you both had a chance to say goodbye. You know she's not trapped in time now. She's at peace, Dae. It was good what you did. I'm sorry I ever said anything."

"That doesn't matter right now." I went inside and put the sheets in the wash. Each movement was painful with loss. Maybe I had said goodbye, but I wasn't ready to let go.

Kevin wanted to take me out for dinner. I wasn't up for that or the questions that would be involved. I didn't want to think about the answers. I just wanted to stay home.

"Okay." He kissed me. "I could bring some food from the Blue Whale. We could eat here. I don't want to leave you alone like this."

I smiled, but I wanted to be alone and told him so. He left after dozens of protests, and I promised to call him as soon as I felt better.

When he was gone, I grew restless. Despite my original thoughts that I wanted to be home, I put my shoes back on and went out.

It was raining, the warm summer rain that we used to play in as kids. My mother used to tell me that it was okay as long as I didn't see any lightning. I used to wait until I had seen lightning a few times before I actually went back inside. It had to get close to the house before it scared me.

There was no lightning or thunder that night. Even the sound was calm despite the rain. The lights were off on the boardwalk—probably a glitch of some kind—they happened often. I could still see the sandbar from the lights at Wild Stallions. Inside, people were laughing and enjoying themselves. I was glad I wasn't with them.

I thought my eyes were playing tricks on me when I saw someone on the sandbar. Then I thought it was Cathi, waiting for her lover. But the figure was too small, too thin, to be Cathi. It made me wonder if someone had lost a child.

Swinging down from the boardwalk, I walked carefully along the edge of the sandbar until I reached the figure. Her white hair was blown wildly by the breeze, and her feet were bare. I'd never seen Mrs. Euly Stanley so disheveled.

"Mrs. Stanley?"

"Oh." She looked up at me. "Dae. It's you."

"How did you get down here? Do you need help getting back up on the boardwalk?"

I knew she couldn't even weigh a hundred pounds. Her dress was damp from the water. I couldn't tell what color it was in the dim light. Maybe I could get her back up by myself. If not there were plenty of able bodies in the restaurant.

"No. I'm fine." She smiled. "I won't be here for long anyway. I'm leaving tonight."

"Where are you going?" Had she hit her head or something?

"I'm going with the only man I've ever loved. You remember the story I told you. The one thing I left out was his name—Tovi." She chuckled. "All this time, and he still remembers me, even though I don't look a thing like I used to. He still loves me too. I'm going to swim with him. I'm ready."

I didn't want to be the one to tell her that he was with Cathi. What had Tovi said to her? Or had she imagined it out of her past? Mrs. Stanley was never the imaginative dreamer who might be standing on the sandbar waiting for her merman lover to appear.

I was at a loss to know what to do.

"Oh. I brought this with me." She held up the gold-handled cane she used to get around with. "You should take it with you, Dae. I'm sure it will answer questions about Captain Lucky and his unfortunate fate, both for you and the medical examiner."

I took it from her, and immediately years of experience flooded through me beginning with where the cane had been made. It also showed me Captain Lucky's death.

"I'm so sorry that it came to it," she said. "He was a lovely man but exceptionally greedy. I asked him to destroy the pictures he had of Tovi and his sister. He laughed at me. I wouldn't let him expose them. So when he turned to go back to the Andalusia, I gave him a whack on the head. He fell into the water. Tovi pulled him out, but it was too late. That was when I asked him to take me with him. I can't tell you what a joyous moment it was when he said yes."

"You killed Captain Lucky?" I was having a tough time imagining it, even though I had clearly seen what had happened from the cane. "How did you get him back to the ship and make everything so wet?"

"Tovi took him. He'd do anything for me. I opened the windows in the stateroom, and Tovi and his sister splashed gallons of water inside. It seemed a fitting end for Captain Lucky."

There was a splash close beside us, and Tovi's face appeared in the water.

"Are you ready, Euly?"

She held out her hand to him. "I've waited all my life for you."

"Maybe you should think about this." I tried to caution.

But it was too late. She jumped into the water, and it closed over her head. I started to dive in after her when I saw Tovi with her in his arms. I couldn't keep my mouth from hanging open.

"Goodbye, Dae." She waved to me. "Always follow your heart."

Those were the last words she spoke to me. With a powerful flick of his beautiful blue and orange tail, Tovi and Mrs. Euly Stanley were gone.

Epilogue

It was a month after Mrs. Stanley disappeared that we held her memorial on the sandbar. We did a short memorial for Captain Lucky, but he was from Portsmouth, Virginia and his body had been shipped there for his official funeral.

Mrs. Stanley had been well-organized about her passing. Everything the police needed to know was clearly identified and written down for them. Her affairs were in order, even down to the memorial she wanted on the sandbar and her final bequest to the town.

Only ten people could stand on the sandbar at one time, but hundreds were on the boardwalk, leaning over the rail, and seated on the wood stairs that led down to the water.

Mrs. Stanley's daughter, Evelyn, had come back home for the memorial. She was clearly embarrassed by her mother's death and confession to murder. She'd brought her husband and son with her. It was the first time in years that Evelyn had come to visit her mother.

At a signal from Chris Slayton, I began to read from the memorial speech I'd written for her.

"We're here today to honor one of the true Bankers, Mrs. Euly Stanley. Her last wish was that we would install this sign on the sandbar."

Chris held it up. It was a small image of a smiling mermaid. Beside it were the words — "*Mer-Safe Haven.*"

Everyone applauded.

"Mrs. Stanley left the town a yearly endowment to make sure that mermaids and mermen aren't persecuted here in Duck. We honor her memory today by placing her sign here and blowing the coral horn to make sure all seafolk know they have safe passage."

Tess had gone home to Minnesota after Tovi and Lilly had left Duck, but she'd come back for the memorial when I asked her to blow the horn. She took a deep breath and blew hard into it. The sound was deep and low, echoing around us, making everyone present shiver when they heard it.

After she'd blown into it, Mark Samson took possession of the coral horn. Captain Lucky had no relatives that we could find to pass it down to, so I used my rights as the person who'd paid for it to donate it to the museum.

A storm was coming up at the horizon. The sky was dark, and the winds were making the swells on the Currituck Sound larger. I suggested that we all adjourn for drinks at Wild Stallions to honor Mrs. Stanley. The crowd began slowly moving in that direction.

Cathi waited for me to climb off the sandbar. Her eyes were misty as she looked out at the water.

"I'm sorry he didn't take you with him," I said when we were alone.

"They'll be back, Dae." She smiled. "I understand his love for Mrs. Stanley. Next time, I'll go with them too."

She didn't go toward Wild Stallions, instead leaving the boardwalk, heading home.

There was a large splash. I turned my head quickly, not in time to see what could have caused it. But there were blue, gold, and orange scales on the sign post which hadn't been put in the sand yet.

I heard the sound of laughter in the distance and went to join Kevin and my friends for a drink.

About the Authors

Joyce and Jim Lavene write bestselling mystery together. They have written and published more than 70 novels for Harlequin, Berkley and Gallery Books along with hundreds of non-fiction articles for national and regional publications.

Pseudonyms include J.J. Cook, Ellie Grant, Joye Ames and Elyssa Henry

They live in rural North Carolina with their family, their rescue animals, Quincy - cat, Stan Lee - cat and Rudi - dog. They enjoy photography, watercolor, gardening and long drives

Visit them at **www.joyceandjimlavene.com**
www.Facebook.com/JoyceandJimLavene
Twitter: **https://twitter.com/AuthorJLavene**
Amazon Author Central Page: **http://amazon.com/author/jlavene**